Sit a Tall Horse

Stories of Cowhand Give & Take

Paul H

Sit a Tall Horse
Paul Hunter
copyright @ 2020 Paul Hunter

All rights reserved including those of translation. This book, or parts thereof, may not be reproduced in any form without the written permission of the author or publisher. Neither the author nor publisher, by publication of this material, ensure to anyone the use of such material against liability of any kind including infringement of any patent. Inquiries should be addressed to the publisher, Davila Art & Books LLC.

Publisher
Davila Art & Books LLC.
PO Box 1627 Sisters, Oregon 97759
541-549-2064

ISBN 978-1-885210-33-3

Also by Paul Hunter

Clownery (2017)
Stubble Field (2012)
One Seed to Another (2010)
Come the Harvest (2008)
Ripening (2007)
Breaking Ground (2004)
Clown Car (2000)
Lay of the Land (1997)
Mockingbird (1981)
Pullman (1976)
Your House is on Fire and your
Children Are Gone (1970)

"Against the Spin of the World" first appeared in Small Farmer's Journal

(Volume 42, No. 3)

"Stumble-Step" appeared in Small Farmer's Journal (Volume 42, No. 4)

The image on the front cover appeared, without signature or credit, in a depression era farm magazine. If anyone should know the artist's name, the author would appreciate learning of it.
On the back cover: "Matador, Texas, 1890" from the Library of Congress.
"Cowboys and Campfire Stories."

For Lynn R. Miller
true horseman

A decent cowboy does not take what belongs to someone else, and if he does he deserves to be strung up and left for the flies and coyotes.
　　　- Judge Roy Bean

There is something about riding on a prancing horse that makes you feel like something, even when you ain't worth a thing.
　　　- Will Rogers

Blame it or praise it, there is no denying the wild horse in us.
　　　- Virginia Woolf

A goodlookin horse is like a goodlookin woman… They're always more trouble than what they're worth. What a man needs is just one that will get the job done.
　　　- Cormac McCarthy

The spirit is near, yet all but invisible. Don't be the rider who gallops all night and never sees the horse that carries him.
　　　- Rumi

Contents

Mama's Boy   7
Burnt Crow   13
Vagabundos   19
Standing on His Reins   27
Dark Like the Lid Shut on Everything   35
The Genuine Article   45
Cowboy Love   51
Trail Talk   59
Dingus   65
Back-Country Justice   71
Blindered Ambition   77
Riding Half a Dream Horse   87
Out Along the Ragged Edge   95
Feeling Halfway Home   103
Night Watch   113
Stumble-Step   121
The First Knowing and the Last   133
Against the Spin of the World   143

Mama's Boy

Out on the range sometimes up in the hills that we only get around
to twice a year, come spring drive you will sometimes find you a big ol'
mama's boy. Bullcalf dropped out of reach in the back country, missed last
spring somehow, then again last fall, hid away most likely, now a yearling
still on the teat, bigger than his mama, down on his knees. Heisting her
way up in the air to get fed. Sometimes he just gets too big too quick, then
mama can't do much about it. A sight to behold, that only goes to show if
some weren't forced they never would let go.

This time a couple of the boys took it as their duty to wean him on the
spot. Got a couple lassos on the big boy and dragged him away still bawling after her. Rubbed cayenne pepper, mustard and Vaseline, whatall we
had in the mess kit, all over the mama's bag to kill the taste. Staked him
out for the night near the string of ponies. But he never would shut up. And
in spite of the hobbles she kept coming for him till they tossed a line on
her too, staked her out the far side of the camp. Their back-and-forth duet
that night got pretty old, and nobody got much shut-eye. But what are you
gonna do? They call this a cow-calf operation, even with seven hundred
eighty some odd square miles that's really all it is. It's not their fault that
they got overlooked in scrub hills and canyons that run away forever, where
you could lose Pancho Villa's raggedy army or a scalded jet plane down in
flames.

Besides which he had to get hungry enough to eat grass. Which was
sparse at the moment, though his mama somehow found enough to feed
them both. And lucky her boy was pretty tame, didn't yet know his own
strength or he mighta been a real handful. When we stirred at sunup, there
was no surprise, the bullcalf had got loose, and they were back together, the
big boy nursing away, making hardly a sound.

But, sleep or not, things can look different by the light of day. With
coffee and biscuits, cackleberries and bacon in us, nobody seemed so hot
to split up that cow and calf. With more'n a thousand pounds of determi-

nation to him, we'd mostly just as soon leave that mama's boy alone, just bring the two of them in as kind of a bonus, along with the 212 new calves and their mamas we'd found. Not as good as some years, but not so bad really. And for now that was that. We'd let ol' Lionel Kendricks and his foreman see what they thought, since it was their worry, their spread and their stock. A couple of the older pokes thought all that milk might offset the gamey taste of bull, and they might be right. Likely worth a shot.

So we put a halter and lead onto mama, and her bullcalf followed right along. After a long day of slow drag and hurry up, by nightfall we had all the new calves and their mamas shut in the big corral below the bunkhouse, ready for shots and tagging next morning.

I'm an early riser, as befits my station like to wake up slow, so first thing I notice old Lionel Kendricks up early too, toddling down to the corral, coffee in hand, to see what we had fetched, like it was Christmas—or more likely Easter, what with the balmy weather, the pollen and hum in the air, the larks just a-goin'it.

Bald old Lionel had on his creamy brandnew Stetson cocked like Sunday-go-to-meeting, staring in at that cow with her big ol' bullcalf balancing her on his nose to get his breakfast. Saying Well, will you looka that. Like he'd never seen such a thing, where we all know good and well on a place like this if he was looking he coulda seen such a thing every three-four years. But I was forgetting something, as I stood there alongside the boss, blowing into my coffee. I forgot who I was talking to, since I hardly ever saw Lionel Kendricks to nod to anyhow. I had no idea what he thought of me. Just another one of the hands I suppose. Ben Wilder the grizzly old guy said to be a top hand. And now here he was. So I pointed to the bullcalf about his business and said Will ya look at that mama's boy.

Ol' Lionel says What'd you say? I sez He's a mama's boy, which is purely all he is.

He scrunched up his face like his teeth hurt, and I rethought my remark. Lionel had never married, was his mother's constant escort and companion till she died a few years back in her mid-90s. Eleanor Lowell Kendricks had been a widow since her husband Gander Kendricks slid out of the saddle into an early grave in his mid-50s, some kind of a massive heart thing while we were out mending fence and nowhere near a phone.

I'd been just a boy then, but already knew he'd been the real thing, ran the place his granddaddy had homesteaded way back when. Over the years we'd been given to understand that the old lady had a nice house up in Boston and another in New Orleans, where she preferred to spend each fall and spring. She had a daughter Lucille ten years younger than Lionel, who had an accountant husband and two young boys, lived several hours away in a suburb of Fort Worth. They'd drive out to the ranch for picnics and holidays, mostly when the old lady and her son were home, every winter and summer for years. After his mother's funeral Lionel had announced he was done gallivanting around, didn't see the sense to it, besides which he liked it fine on the place, where he could run in to Houston or Dallas in his Escalade when he needed a break from the red dust and chiggers and horse-flies. Nowadays when you can get practically anything on the cable TV, your secret heart's desire, between that and the deep freeze and air conditioning they were just about shut of hardluck ranching anyhow.

So as the boys filed out of the bunkhouse into the bright sun rubbing their heads, Lionel leans over and asks when we get to the branding. I say Not much branding to be done today. These calves will just get ear-tags, unless they get picked out for breeding stock. We still brand the keepers. There I stop, since Lionel oughta know all this. Broke horses and breeding stock still wear the K- Bar on the left rump, plus ol' Dockerty, the pack mule named for our one-eyed trail cook who died the year he was born, that must be 35 if he's a day. We still take him along on roundups because he hardly has to be led or tied. He would follow us anywhere, but we don't like to load him down much these days. Ol' Dock's got plenty on his pack frame what with coffeepot, plates and cups, Dutch ovens and skillets.

Tags? Oh, yeah, ear-tags, I get it, what was I thinking of.

Lionel can sit a horse pretty good if he doesn't have to go far. He has a smooth easy side, and a prickly side. He can be real pleasant, lay out for a serious spread at a party, hire a string band and dance with all the ladies anybody brought. But if he thought someone was being critical he could be worse than a mess of cholla cactus past midnight. And since his schooling time away at Dartmouth thirty years ago he has yet to do a lick of work.

Just then the foreman Len Dawes calls the boys together over on the porch, to line out the day, see who's doing what. And I see there might

be another problem. They'll be castrating bullcalves here with the owner
around.

Right away a couple of the boys start in about who's got dibs on the
prairie oysters, argue about the good eating, how to fix 'em right. They
don't quit, though I give 'em both the eye. But Lionel leaning on the top
rail pays no mind to the boys, still watching that big baby nursing away
across the corral. Then when the boys drift apart, Len shows up at his
elbow, says good morning, seems to have something on his mind.

I see you spotted that bullcalf the boys found.

Yeah. Something else, ain't he.

What do you have a mind to do with him?

Well, he's a bull, ain't he.

Scrub bull. We got too many a them as it is.

Scrub? Looks pretty healthy to me.

Look at them shoulders. That short back. He don't have no real size to
him. Nor no size to his business. That's how you tell, just look between his
legs.

What are you sayin'?

We can't send him to market like he is. Wouldn't fetch nothing. Have
to fix him first, then feed him up a while. Or we could call the slaughter
truck, dress him out here for the freezer, to eat on the place. Some of the
boys say what with all that milk, his meat might not be so bad.

Len looks off and spits into the corral. He expects Lionel to say That's
a thought, and leave it for him to decide. But Lionel is wagging his head a
little, dug in about something. He won't be pushed, and Len can't for the
life of him see what it is.

'Course, if you got another idea.

Lionel doesn't say a word, won't look his foreman in the eye. They just
stand next to each other looking off. The boys are getting set up for the
work now, carrying a picnic table over next to the squeeze gate they'll be
running the calves through. Setting out the box of ear tags and all those
special pliers. A bucket for the oysters. First a calf gets a number, then
comes the rest of it. The clipboard with the shot records and syringes and a
cooler with the medicines.

It doesn't look so bad. In the corral the calves are still quiet, oblivious. If they think anything, they figure out the other end they'll get their mamas back. But this is where it's decided. From here on their lives all open one way out. The jaws of that gate might as well be the mouth of the wicked old world, that opens and shuts and in-between chews on us all. Some think they get to play god, though it's a test of character not to pass on the living as profit or loss, and let a little of the wild get by.

So what do you want to do? Len slowly turns to face him, hard as leather, windburned, calm.

What's that my old man liked to say? Just 'cause you trim his ears back, don't make a horse of a mule.

Len says I don't take your point.

Do we have to do this now?

Now is when we're here, set up to get done. So what's your pleasure?

Lionel looks up, down, sideways. Says Why can't you just leave him be?

It's a muttered outcry, half-swallowed, pathetic. There's the cow up-lifted by her ungainly, outrageous child. Len suddenly looks hopeless as a snowman on a stove. He sees Lionel is not gonna make the call, turns and stares at me. He's like the horses on the place, mostly don't want to look you in the eye, so when he does there's something up. A top hand never ducks a look, or shirks the dirty work. In a second or two I know what's got to be done, and give him the nod. And watch Kendricks out of the corner of my eye shake the grounds out of his cup, swivel on his boot heel and head back up to the big house.

Then I remember something else. How quick the old place changed once that old lady died. A woman who as a little girl had heard Teddy Roosevelt give a speech, said she could have heard him talk forever, though she hardly garnered a word. All her antique furniture, art deco statues and stuff, potted palms and beaded fringes from the 20s, all the fancy red and blue and green leather-bound books, that Lionel had us boys box up, bundle into a stock trailer and haul to an antique dealer he knew in Santa Fe. There had been some hard feelings but he'd just rammed it through. The distant kin could be ignored, but his sister Lucille had wanted some of those things, had really wanted the home place to stay just like it was, not a button undone, so she could come visit, bring her boys and feel like part of something bigger and finer and grander than she'd ever been or known.

She hadn't gotten along with her mother like Lionel had, two of a kind that always knew what was best, and now had her own to take care of. And as for Lionel, well, anybody could see how things stood. To his way of thinking he'd already given half a life, and now was set to live the other half.

There's not much more to tell. After lights-out I saddled up Jericho and threw a loop over the bullcalf, dragged him out and had my pony back and hold him while I shut the gate on his mama. Rode a couple hours south by half a moon, listening to the cool night full of that sweet racket all around. Mourning doves and peepers and whatnot. Stayed far away from the fragrant trail we had trampled on the drive coming in. Tied that bullcalf up to a juniper with a piece of rotten old rope I already knew he could break once he got around to trying. Shook a couple flakes of clover hay out of a garbage bag under his nose, left the last of it a couple feet out of reach, then rode off south in the dark another hour before I circled round to the east, to get the benefit of the sunrise heading home.

As for that mama's boy, he quit bawling before I was out of earshot. Hard to bawl in the dark when you crave to hear what's going on, with nothing else out there but nightjars and coyotes and such to call or answer back. We'd like to think he had a rough start, being born without us. But he had a smart mama with a knack for hiding them both. Now he'll find his way. He's a good enough size nothing much'll bother him. As far as how he turns out, I guess we're gonna see.

Burnt Crow

Back when the world was young with me on the run, I got a cook job
on the Lazy B because nobody wanted it. Vern the regular cook slipped on
frosty planks out front of the cook house ringing the breakfast bell, skidded
off the porch and broke an ankle, so couldn't make the fall drive. Almost a
paid vacation, to hear the boys tell it, to hobble around with a crutch and
a cast and your naked toes blue in the breeze, with a peg on the bottom so
you could spin around and snatch biscuits out of the oven one-handed.

Cooking is usually not all that hard, though it can be a whole lot of
thankless. But providing you stick to simple stuff, and don't mind poking
around in a recipe book, you can pick it up. Miles from nowhere you have
to make sure you packed what you need, got that yeast and salt, butter,
flour, baking powder, salsa, tins of molasses and a keg of sourdough starter,
and aren't afraid to wing it a little. With a Dutch oven or three hot all at
once you can bake chicken and biscuits and beans. With a grill you can
barbecue and stir some sauce to slather on. What I did was pretty simple
stuff—chili, rump roast with onions, potatoes and carrots, biscuits and
gravy, flapjacks, maybe apple cobbler, depending what was on hand, if I
still had any syrup. But I had the right kind of eaters, after a long day in the
saddle ornery as buzzards and not too particular, providing the grub was
hot right now and plenty of it.

One trouble I had right away, was too many bosses. The foreman liked
his coffee at sunup, which out on the drive meant I had to be up most of an
hour before to build a fire and get the big pot on, that took forever to boil.
Learned to put on a little pot first so his never had to wait. But then the
boys whose turn it was to feed and water stock wanted their coffee the minute they got up too, and I had to tell them coffee was at sunup not before.
Which some days got me to feeling like there was no winning for losing,
and someone would always be grumpy.

But the cooking was a bounty in itself. When the boys lined up with their tin plates full of beans and I'd ask how they wanted their steak, listen good then spear them one that looked pink or red or charred enough to be perfect, it felt like I'd made a friend for life—or at least until breakfast. The boys didn't mind a little eggshell in their coffee, and were not given to phony compliments.

I'd been Vern's dishwasher handyman for a month when his ankle broke, and only had a few days to get my own footing before we headed up in the hills to hunt and herd cattle. Apropos of nothing, Vern liked to quote Abraham Lincoln, who is supposed to have said Just because the cat has her kittens in the oven, that don't make 'em biscuits. To balance such unlikely wisdom I had Mutt and Jeff, a skinny young pair of mules to hitch to the chuckwagon, which was a pretty decent portable kitchen, though on that roundup I also learned it had mice, that could eat their way into practically anything—but that's another story. Vern had told me I should roll out my bag under the wagon to keep down pilfering, stand my ground and let them know who was boss, of the chuckwagon anyhow. But I was seventeen, who was I kidding. Cook was a job for a greenhorn, until somebody came along who couldn't sit a saddle anymore, so somehow had to put up with it.

Which wasn't me but so what. The first thing that took a while to figure on my own was that the boys wanted what they were used to, what they got every day. They hated anything new. They even wanted what they had to complain about. Nobody much cared what they got, providing things went about like they were supposed to. Whether they got their bacon a little burnt or a little rubbery, it gave them something to grouse about while they were still half-asleep.

Some things were sacred. I made coffee like always, hot and strong and bitter, with a pinch of salt, a couple eggshells and a splash of cold water to settle the grounds, with a bag of sugar and a carton of milk sitting handy for those prone to doctoring theirs.

But I did feel like I was missing out, stuck in camp every day, except when we got the word to move. Then I'd have to tie down my pots and harness Mutt and Jeff, and follow somebody who knew where they were going, since there was no map and anyhow the boys all knew these hills. I had never driven a team before, or really worked mules. So that first time I got Vern to hop around and show me where all the straps and buckles went. Got so I watched their ears to see what they were paying attention to, moved slow around them, and talked a little nonsense while I was harnessing. I never did get directions from anybody else, just clicked my tongue and slapped the reins like the old-timers did, and they went right along.

Mutt and Jeff taught me a lot. As long as I wasn't having a bad day neither were they. They didn't like to be forced into anything, especially muddy water, but would look it over, then could usually be led. And since we were in charge of the chuckwagon, just to sweeten the deal they got a treat now and then.

After a hot dry summer, it was getting to be a damp fall, so to give the boys a little something special I got the idea of going mushroom hunting. My cousin Mayellen in San Angelo had learned from her grandmother how to tell a mushroom from a toadstool, and which were the good eating ones. Though her husband Clyde didn't care for me one bit, she did what she could. One fall day we were out on a picnic in the country, and we took a walk in the woods where she showed me how to find several different kinds, which mostly meant looking for several kinds of dead and dying trees. Clyde was sitting in the shade on a blanket, drinking beer and yelling at her, sounding jealous and childish. So pitiful for a minute there I almost felt bad for him.

As the roundup was winding down, I had a couple hours off in late morning, since most of the boys would be gone till suppertime. So I made up a big pot of soup, corn and beans, peppers and onions with bay leaves and a ham hock, set it at the edge of the fire with the lid on. Then put out a pile of bowls and spoons on the tailgate, for whoever might drift in and feel peckish. Then I untied Mutt and rode him on a gunny sack up into the hills to see if the mushrooms were showing.

Conditions looked about right so I kept looking but for the longest
time didn't spot a one. But then right when I was set to give it up and turn
around, there was a little one, just poking out of the ground, and then some
more, a kind I remembered from Mayellen, though I couldn't remember
the name. Looked like a brain on a stem. Along one shady hillside there
they set, working up through the dead leaves and tangle underfoot, march-
ing along like she'd said, like little soldiers with their heads up in the cool
damp air. I slipped down from Mutt, tied him a little ways off, and started
filling my gunnysack. Took me half an hour to get a bushel, then I climbed
aboard and headed back to camp.

I didn't really have a plan, though I knew enough not to say a thing.
Figured to surprise 'em I might bake a casserole, some kind of a side dish
with sliced potatoes and cheese, peppers and onions, then slip the mushrooms in before anybody noticed. Which is what I did. The Dutch oven
had about done bubbling and I'd put the cheese on top, stirred and covered
it in before the sun got too low and the boys started trickling in. I had a
heap of barbecued ribs going, and a big pot of rice. Around the fire pretty
soon they were all watching with interest as I poked and slathered and
turned.

When I said the magic words— Get you a plate, Come and get it—
things looked like they might be fine. I started dishing up the casserole
and rice, and spearing them some ribs. Then a minute later the first hand
says What is this? I look at his fork and says That's a mushroom. There was
a thin rattle of laughter round the fire like sleet on the bunkhouse roof.
I might as well have said poison, since from then on no one would touch
that casserole, no one would eat a bite. I didn't say a word, just picked out a
couple raw ones from my sack, shook off the dirt and wolfed them down in
front of everyone. If I'd been a vaquero, they might have tried a little just to
humor me, but I was a kid after all, the youngest one here, and there were
no Mexicans on the place who might know and say different. So they ate all
the ribs, and I was stuck eating casserole like it was burnt crow.

Next morning after everyone else had their breakfast, after I'd scraped and stacked the plates and put some wash water on, I chopped up the last of the mushrooms and stirred them into my eggs, and sat there eating as they shook out the grounds in their cups, saddled up and rode off.

On the trail home I had a lot of quiet miles to think it over. There's a thing about cooking, everybody knows. They'd a loved me if I'd a baked cookies. They say the way to a man's heart is through his stomach. But for the life of me I can't remember a thing my mother ever cooked, except for my school lunches back in Fresno, baloney and cheese on white bread with mayo wrapped in waxed paper, with an orange or apple. Every day identical. After my dad died, I hardly ever ate another baloney and cheese, or another piece of fruit till I was out on my own.

When we got back from the drive and caught up on our sleep, one morning I had a word with the foreman. This was back when I still thought jobs grew on trees. Told him I was thinking over this cooking deal, and didn't like being responsible for anybody else's happiness. He says Happiness, to hear the sound of it, and laughs. Says Who do you think you are, Sandy Claus? I said Maybe that's just the kid in me, but it was the kid in them too, it was that simple. In the end I could see the hands deserved to eat and needed to eat, and that was a job that needed done so I'd do it. But if I was going to keep doing it, I would have to like it, and I didn't, so when Vern's foot was good enough to let him really cook again, I was set to move on. The foreman says Looky here, Ben. You think you're better at cooking than Vern? I says It's only a matter of time. I may be just a kid, but Vern never puts a thing in his mouth that he cooks, and I can't help but taste everything.

Vagabundos

There were two speckled live hens tied together with twine by the
claws, slung upside-down across the taller vaquero's saddle-horn, as they
rode into the yard. Maybe he was no taller, just wore a taller hat, sat a taller
horse, or sat up straight. Clearly the leader, a little older and a touch more
serious. The chickens would occasionally panic and flutter. One would start
up, then both swirl a miniature blizzard, that soon wore itself out and fell
quiet. Maybe it was just to save their strength. Or maybe they went limp
with despair or forgetting. Neither of the horses seemed much bothered by
these dusty, feathery outbursts, though the smaller rider grinned. Out with
a bucket of kitchen slops for the pigs, I watched the two vaqueros approach,
with the thought I might be seeing freshly stolen dinner on the hoof.

Buenos dias.

I raised my hand in greeting, said Buenos dias in return.

Por favor, do you know of a place, un campamento, where we might
rest for the night?

Here on the Lazy B it was only late morning. Their gear was timeless,
worn and mended. The bridles and reins of both horses had been pieced
and patched, stitched and riveted. The cantle of the younger vaquero's
saddle was worn away to the wood. Both had bedrolls and slickers and
saddlebags, the taller one with a small satchel tied on behind him while the
younger had a cotton flour sack. The one without the chickens also had a
fair-sized pot hanging off his rig, ringing against a little metal something I
couldn't see. I eyed the near chicken, who for the moment eyed me back.
I pointed out the dusty gravel lane they had just ridden in, and said You
turn left out at the road. There is a cottonwood grove to the west, by the
big bend in the creek. Not far. A mile and a half. You are welcome to camp
there.

Muchos gracias.

You must have come from the east.

Verdad, that is so.

Do you mind me asking how you come by the chickens?

At sunup we came upon some cows out along the road. We drove them back in, found a fencepost had rotted and fallen. So we set it back up and braced it. The old couple who came out to watch us caught up these birds, and offered them as a gift.

They are fine-looking birds.

Yes. A shame we have no safe way to keep them.

Then the taller one with the chickens said The water there—what is it like?

The horses will like it. A little muddy, but sweet.

With that the two men said Gracias again, nodded and waved, then turned their horses and headed back out toward the road still quiet and hidden from the yard.

I wondered which neighbor the chickens had come from. They wouldn't last too long on the road in the hot sun. So it must have been one of the near neighbors, and only a short while ago. I kept thinking about them as I did my chores, scrubbed the pans and dishes from breakfast, then helped Vern the cook get supper going, hobbling around on his broken ankle in a walking cast. But I kept thinking about those two men, so polite and straightforward, yet private. I felt a little guilty suspecting they might be thieves. So after I peeled and chopped and had things set for supper, I took a break, put a handful of carrots and potatoes and onions and a stick of butter in a paper bag, and said I'm going out to give Cindy a ride.

Then I went down to the corral and saddled my mare. She was glad to see me, and made a show of inspecting my pockets. I broke her off a chunk of carrot, then walked her through the gate, closed it and stepped up. We gathered ourselves, rode out the drive to the road and headed west. And twenty minutes later, down at the bend in the creek there they were, both horses unsaddled and staked out. The leader was sitting with his back against the largest old tree, drawing in a sketch pad. At least that's what I thought he was doing. I'd never seen a real person do that, who wasn't a schoolteacher, or a kid with a crayon. The other man was downstream a couple hundred yards. I couldn't see for sure what he was doing.

Buenos tardes.

He looked up, smiled and nodded. I stepped down and tied Cindy to a nearby tree. Then I brought my paper bag along, walked over to the man, and introduced myself.

I forgot my manners earlier. My name is Ben Wilder.

He looked up but didn't move. He put his hand to his chest to say his name, Hernan Gonzales.

I bent down to shake his hand, and said I brought you some things to go with your chickens. I work with the cook on the place.

When I handed him the bag he slowly opened it and shyly peeked in. And smiled for the first time, said Gracias. Said Roderigo is plucking the chickens. He pointed downstream to where I could see the other man crouched over something.

Do you mind if I see what you're drawing?

Hernan turned his sketchpad around to show me. I hunkered down for a look. There were half a dozen sketches of the two chickens on the first page he showed, starting with one of the pair hanging upside down from his pommel, with the twine at their ankles. Then came several of them confused and dazed on the ground together, looking around, getting their bearings, each still with the knotted twine on one foot tethering it to the other bird. Then several sketches of them calmly pecking at small bugs and plants underfoot. The sketches became a trail of little moments in their lives. The two birds were shaded and touched by the soft dark pencil, like shadows that reached out and led back to his own dark eye. The last drawing showed a complicated dance of awareness. Each of the birds was watching what the other was finding even as she hunted for herself. Between them was a wordless little dialogue, questions flung back and forth. What are you finding? Is there something better hiding there?

I nodded and looked at him. These are very fine. Alive.

Hernan nodded, smiled. Said But now they are no more. Only moments gone, now all we have are scribbles.

And supper.

With that he looked up at Roderigo, now standing a few steps off, holding the two plucked hens by the claws, each headless neck still dripping faint pink drops on the gravel. Standing there with the naked bodies he seemed nearly as young and oblivious as I felt at seventeen.

Hernan made introductions, said my name. Then he said Roderigo
agreed if I would kill and clean the birds then he would pluck them. But I
needed to draw them first.

How about if I cook them for you? I have to get back to make dinner,
but could at least get your meal going.

Hernan said It would be an honor.

I saw that the big pot had been used to boil coffee, balanced on a small
grill over several stones. And that they had a lid for it. I added some twigs
under the pot and stirred the fire, then poured the last of the coffee into
their cups. I rinsed the pot at the creek, put the stick of butter in, opened
my knife and set to work cutting up the two hens.

Do you have seasonings?

Salt and pepper and some dried chilis.

Perfecto.

In went the pieces of chicken, that I seasoned, turned and browned
with my knife. Then in went the onions to brown quickly, followed by
potatoes and carrots, with enough water to cover. Then I put on the lid, and
pulled the pot back to where it would simmer slowly.

As I straightened up and turned to go, Hernan says Muchas gracias.

De nada. Perhaps I will see you in the morning, if you are still here.

Come have coffee with us. It would be an honor.

Maybe too late for you.

Hernan and Roderigo both laughed.

What is the joke?

Amigo, we are at liberty. Free as the breeze.

Vagabundos?

Exactamente.

In the morning I couldn't wait to get to the camp by the creek. I
cooked us three piles of flapjacks that I put in pie tins, hurried though the
cleanup after the hands had eaten and left. I brought another stick of butter and a bottle of syrup in a paper bag. Cindy checked me over for treats,
found her apple and got to munch it while I saddled her for the ride.

And there we were again. They had strung a tarp to sleep under, for
shelter and shade. Hernan was sketching again. I wondered why I was here,

bothering them, and instantly knew I was here to see how he did it, how he captured the life on the fly. It was like no other work I had seen, no dance I could imagine.

When I stepped close and greeted him, he reached up to take my hand. Then as if to answer what I had not asked, he turned the pad around and handed it to me. There were several new sketches of their horses, across the clearing, tied to a picket line. The two horses seemed familiar and companionable. The best of the drawings showed their momentary game of attention. His gelding studied something in the distance, perhaps a sound he hadn't yet spotted the source of, while the other lifted and turned her head, curious to take it in. There were also a couple of drawings of the tree where he usually sat, seen from where the horses were. He took in the tarp and its lines but made those human touches feel faint and ghostly. In each drawing of the big cottonwood Hernan's pencil was restless, touching something behind the stillness, pulling a presence out of its heavy old limbs that seemed to soar, scattering patches of light and shade.

These were surprising. Something in the tree stirring, catching at the eye.

Then I said Could I see you draw one from the start?

Of course. But just a little. We don't want the food to get cold. With that he poured me coffee into his own cup, took back the pad, settled himself against the tree, and looked around. He started on a sketch of Cindy, who was tied on the line with their horses. No sooner had he laid down one strong line of her back and shoulder, her head down to graze, than she lifted her head, aware that Hernan was studying her.

Turning his eyes from her, he said A special mare.

Yes, she is. Always watching everything. Does that make her hard to draw?

No, she will relax once she decides I mean no harm. With that he turned the page and started another sketch, of all three horses. Seeing something, working quickly to catch it all before it changed.

How do you get all the…sizes? I don't know what to call it.

Proporcionado? Much practice. I am like a tailor, always measuring, always checking the fit.

Do you do this a lot? Do you live on the road?

No, only when work is slow on the place. We ride for two or three weeks, go wandering to see what is out here. Then one day it is enough, we turn for home. Back there in a shed I paint what is still there, that is worth a second look, perhaps a little work.

Still there?

Hernan reached deep under the shade of his hat, and tapped the side of his head.

I opened the bag and sat the three pie tins full of flapjacks to warm by the fire. I put big lumps of butter on top, and set out the bottle of syrup. Roderigo approached and thanked me for the chicken stew last night.

The chickens were young and fresh. Hunger is the best sauce.

We laughed, then settled ourselves by the fire. I ask Roderigo if he draws too. He says Not so much, but Hernan says He has a fire in there somewhere, and the younger man ducks his head, pleased but embarrassed. As we ate, I asked questions that had been bothering me since yesterday when I first saw him drawing. When I asked him What is it like to paint a painting, Hernan said What is it like to curry a horse?

I couldn't help but laugh, seeing what he meant. How each time might be different. He said You start anywhere, and go everywhere else till you're done. You never hurry or finish one thing too soon. He said It takes work to know when the painting is finished. Roderigo gravely nodded.

Some painting is more like a maze. You start out lost in something you can't yet see all of, and you press on and if you are lucky, sooner or later you begin to feel your way.

With that Hernan had a question of his own, really a statement. You thought we might be thieves.

The notion crossed my mind. My apologies.

Chicken thieves. Where do you think you got that notion?

You're traveling rough.

What does that mean?

You don't dress up.

And how should we to do that? We carry nothing, hardly a change of clothes. You know what I think? I think you look on the world as an artist too, though you have not yet found your craft. You study us with your questioning eyes—always wide-open, a little suspicious, dubious. Like your Cindy—maybe she gets it from you. Which is only right. Something in the artist must appear to be a thief. Maybe how he eyes the world, learns to take what he can, while he can, in an instant. Even gifts scattered about and ignored, that appear to belong to no one. In such a world even a gift of young hens perfect for the pot might appear to be what it is not.

I notice how careful you are when you watch—people and animals, even things.

Hernan said Like a predator?

Yes.

Training horses and herding cattle we do the same thing. Try not to let them see when I watch, what I am noticing. Try not to startle them with my stare. I think you have already learned that too.

I saw what he meant. Then to change the subject, I told them about the only other painter I know, one of the hands named Tony, who painted his old Ford pickup that spring in swirls, with a lady's powderpuff. Purple, blue, red and gold from head to tail like a rooster in the sunset. How his buddy Lester took one look and said Looks like you used a dead chicken. And Tony said Least I didn't pluck it first.

They both laughed softly. Then I had to go. They were here camping another night, but by the time I got there next morning they were gone. Hernan left a drawing of Cindy and me, riding toward him that first afternoon. It was under the pile of cleaned pie tins, with a rock to keep them from blowing away. I didn't know how I felt about it, though he wrote Muchas gracias on the bottom, and his name.

The sketch is a moment from far down the road, spattered by the light and shade we ride through. Cindy seems focused on him in the distance, ears up, while I look off toward the creek, watching its flow through the trees. Here we are at an easy canter, going the same direction, looking at two different things. Hernan had not even seemed to look up until we were close, and I swung down from the saddle. He might have looked more than once, but may have caught this all in a single sidelong glance.

I liked what I saw, what the drawing offered. Right there and then I got the notion that anything you did could be an art. That the art is what you felt about what you did, that just by doing you might somehow share. That even being some kind of cowboy, working animals without making them fear me, could be a craft and an art—traveling light as I could, with the one pot for everything, that would always feed me, that in turn I always fed.

Standing on His Reins

What kind of a cowhand I make don't much matter. I can break horses,
though I only broke a couple then learned better, thrown once didn't need
to learn that lesson twice. I take my time, and if you don't like it fire me.
I can doctor cows, but I'm always set to look it up in a real book, which I
don't own, or on the internet when I get to run to town, neither of which
nobody owns or should. With a sick animal I'll always call someone that
knows more, a vet should it come to that, before I'd let the critter die, unless it's plain old age.

But what kinda life is it anyhow, where you don't own a thing but your
saddle, the good hat you keep in a box, the everyday hat on a peg while
you're resting indoors, and the upkeep on a couple pair of boots? I don't go
home for the holidays because there's nowhere that'll have me but right here
on the place entirely owned by someone else. Truth to tell, some a these old
boys die in their bunkbeds alone, without sayin' a mumbling word. Around
the place I have a sayso, they may even ask what Ben Wilder thinks, but
that don't come easy. To speak my piece sometimes I have to be set to
quit on the spot. Which they'd let me do in a heartbeat, if I got 'em riled
enough, and said nothing of worth. What else? I don't rodeo, never did.
Most a that's not cowboyin', a show that is anything but. Saw too many
busted up early, left no way to even get around, never mind make a living.
I got no retirement, no security. Sure, there'll be a government check, but
that won't hardly buy hay for some mustang ponies that might still be free,
if I'm quick enough to catch one. When it comes down to it, I figure to
barely buy beans.

That's about the size of it, but for one thing. Consider if you will what I
heard out of this old sailor man Trevor in the Barn Door, a saloon just this
side of Santa Fe, where a bunch of us went and slept in the trailer to catch
a stock auction. Said he'd been round the world by wind power, which
he called a free ride, and I said How'd you manage that? He said I deliver
boats. I wouldn't own a one, they're a hole in the water you throw money

in, but the people who have them need the boat to be where they want it when they want. Half the time the boat is in the wrong place, the wrong side of the puddle, and half the time the weather is blowing the wrong way. No matter where you go there's two ways to go about it, either a downhill sleigh ride or an uphill slog. Which a cowhand like you must know all about. So they hire me, though they're resentful, don't like to pay what it's worth. By the end of that night I asked Trevor why he was here so far from big water, and he said he was trying to see could he break free of it and live without, or what. Which calls to mind a bright young lady I knew once who taught school, couldn't let it go for anything, though those kids were rough and rude. Seventh graders that gave her a hard time of it every day. Which maybe how she secretly liked 'em to start with. Which is about how I feel some dark nights in the cow business. There's things about it you like, that make it tough to quit, though there's a rough side lets you know there's times you'd be better off doing pritnear anything else.

And ever since that night I've thought of something else he said, about how when you're at sea the boat belongs to whoever can work it. Any fool can own a boat on dry land far from water. No fool owns one for long out at sea. That same must hold true for working horses and cattle. They belong to the ones that can work 'em. What else matters?

So much for plain talk and poor mouth. That I have to say day-to-day is mostly bunk. Once you sign on and prove yourself, they let you pick a string of ponies—two, three, four, however many you think you'll need. I had a young gelding colt on this place that I caught and broke and rode same as my own twenty-one years till the morning he stepped on that power line and died. Nobody begrudged him a mouthful, and no one else ever rode him even once. You couldn't buy one that would be any more yours than Apache, do any more that you might think to ask. It's a hard life, but at least it's not a wicked one. And such as the company is and is like to be, you're not alone, though cowhands ain't thick on the ground.

Some places go in for hazing and pranks, where the boys might fool around, especially with greenhorns, snipe hunts and the like, but the Kendricks place wasn't one of those. Mostly straight shooters, with here and there a dope. Which there's no dodging in the long run, I expect. There was plenty of work to be done without making a show of it. And when you're tired enough at night you'll not likely find trouble, that'll have its hands full just shaking you awake.

But about that Apache. Best horse on the place. How could I tell? He was so far out ahead in thinking like a cow, around him they same as did what they were told. Sometimes to think about it I expect I stayed on those twenty-one years just because he wasn't mine. I'd a had to leave the pony, or else pay the man what he was worth. Or carry the saddle without him. Which is a hell of a thing to pack any distance—try to get one on a train or bus or plane—and a royal pain to ship. Only way to get a saddle around is on a horse, where it belongs, rides just right with you setting on it or not. Else in the bed of a pickup, which I also haven't got.

First time I saw him he was standing up on a rock outcrop the far side of the fence that keeps the stock out of the garden, away from the outbuildings and the big house. Nose held up in the wind, head way back. That was his post, where he could see over the bigger older horses up close to the fence, where someone had tossed them a bushel of windfall apples. There he could see what went on with the folks round the place. I was new to the place then, signed on that chilly early spring, just waiting the call in to supper. I went out and climbed the fence, caught up a couple of the apples before the ponies got 'em all, and headed straight for him. I was scouting a decent cow pony, and liked what I saw. He looked smart and quick, not too big not too small, a gelding with a little mustang to him, young enough, standing there with his coat riffling in the wind, a little shaggy and rough. Still had most of his winter coat so must have lately drifted in off the range just like me. I didn't look right at him. I took a bite out of one of those apples, and chewed it with my mouth wide so he could smell it and hear it. When I got close enough I lowered my head as if to look at it, then held it out. And that was it, one big jump off that table rock on the fly here he come, snatched the apple out of my palm, then skidded to a stop a couple yards away, where he stood to eat it, head turned from me. I waited till he was done, then lifted the other apple, took a slow bite and offered it.

That was all it took. For the next week I never saw him without a little something in my pocket, carrot or radish or whatnot, whatever Bixler the Cooky could spare, and he was always standing up there on his perch, where he could see me come out the door of the bunkhouse, and turn his way.

I started working him in the round pen right off. A couple of the hands, Lester and Miguel, had commenced to razz me, said Looks like I'm keeping a pet, stealing treats for it. I didn't bother answering. Besides, what's there to say? No point running your mouth. Working animals, the proof is right there, those that do it best. Which pretty soon anyone standing around with eyes in his head can see.

Besides, I didn't have nothing to tell but what I saw. I didn't grow up around horses or cattle or farming or nothing. My old man Randy Wilder ran an auto body shop in Fresno, made a decent living till he left this life the same day I turned 11, hit by a train at a crossing, hurrying home for dinner with a new bike for me in the trunk. A faulty signal arm they called it, plain hard luck. We three kids were split up, farmed out to various relatives while Mom scouted out another man to make a go of it. She was cute, but a little long in the tooth, as they used to say, and maybe too picky at that point. I was sent to live with one of the cousins she grew up with out in west Texas, in San Angelo. Mayellen Hooper and her husband Clyde. When I was seventeen and come in late from a school dance maybe one in the morning, he smelled beer on me and clocked me, then pulled off his belt and we got into it. That's where my education started and stopped. I hit him with a dishpan full a dirty crockery, and lit out of there before he could clear his head enough to call the cops. For a while I was scared, lost and hungry off and on, though who isn't sometime in their life—but there was never a minute when I thought of going back. Looking for work I drifted north, got on as kitchen helper at a ranch, where I showed I wasn't scared of work and caught on quick. Besides, what they ate there wasn't much. That first day I peeled, boiled and mashed a bushel of potatoes, that were gone in twenty minutes. Pretty soon I was going on drives, cooking up a storm, pokin' round in the recipe books. Picked up riding and roping and driving a team, all a that. The next season I moved on, and at that next place said not a word about the kitchen work, told 'em I was fit to make a top hand some day, which by then I practically was, though I had yet to scrape up enough to buy me a saddle. Said I'd lost mine in a fire, and they lent me an old one that I used for years, wore clean through the hide to the tree.

But I was telling about workin' that pony, wasn't I. I had broke exactly one, on the spread before the one before that, while I was still cooking, just to see could I do it. Took my time, my free hour between breakfast and lunch every day for a week. The old-timers that come in the kitchen for coffee gave me tips, when I could get 'em off one at a time so they weren't just amusin' each other at the greenhorn's expense. First thing I heard was pick a good horse, one with no bad habits, not spoiled yet. Then keep 'em like that, treat 'em right. When I wondered what's the whole point in a nutshell, ol' Pete says, Get 'em to want what you want.

This little mare Cindy looked plenty good enough. The old way of breaking then was to climb aboard and stick till you wore 'em out. The theory was she'd throw you a few times, or a few dozen, then get tired a tryin', and accept you as boss. But Cindy was so smart and so easy, and I was in no hurry, she practically let me know when to stop and go. So we saved a lot a that catchin' and climbin' and throwin' stuff. I led her around with a halter for several days, then with bridle and a saddle blanket, then saddled her a few times, led her around some, then unsaddled her. By the time I showed her what I was gonna do, just spoke to her a little, put my boot in the stirrup, swung up and settled, she gave a little crow-hop sideways, that was it. Didn't even lose my hat. By the time I left the place the boys were practically fighting over who would get Cindy next. I had to threaten 'em with poison biscuits some dark night, if they didn't treat her right.

And now here on the new place was Apache, that had all the stuff a horse could have, and then some. Lotta cow smarts, lotta heart. I only wished we'd met the day his mother dropped him, so we coulda got a head start. I got to be grateful I'd had Cindy, what I'd learned from her, that got me started right. I know, makes it sound like my mother's a horse.

I'd been leading him around the corral, first just a halter, then the saddle blanket, then the bridle, then the saddle cinched on. Curried and brushed him and handled his feet. Mostly I worked a little each morning before breakfast, when there was nobody else much around. Because of the hazing about the treats we were way beyond that, and Apache had gotten away from expecting such things, though he was always excited by a surprise chunk of turnip or apple.

But that morning three of the hands were out by the corral with their coffee in hand, to watch me lead Apache in. And the horse noticed them too. I didn't think much about it at the time, thought I had his complete attention, but it's always worth noticing whatever's new around the animals, and what they make of it.

And I hadn't thought of something else, that only occurred to me later on. But Apache was always watching everything. Anyhow, I had him bridled and saddled, and led him a couple times around the small corral. He was docile, but watching and listening. Then I stopped him on the far side of the ring from the three of them, talked to him a little, low and easy, then slipped my toe into the stirrup, swung my weight up and threw a leg over him.

And sat down hard on the ground. Didn't even click my tongue. He threw me. Ducked his head and threw me hard. Like falling off a roof. And we were to where I'd thought he liked me, so it took a minute to get my head around. I eased up and dusted myself off, but didn't look at him there facing me, standing on his reins a dozen paces off. So was that the kind of a game it was going to be? Maybe I was just in too all-fired of a hurry. I caught up the reins and looked down to where he was standing on them, which as soon as he noticed me spot he danced away a couple steps. I clicked my tongue and led him on around the ring, quiet and easy as you please. When I dropped the reins, he stopped short and stood like he was born to it. I walked over to the far side of the corral, where the three hands were leaning, drinking coffee. I had a notion it was something to do with them, so I turned my back to the horse and talked to them real calm and slow.

Any a you boys ever try to ride this horse? They all shook their heads but Diego was a pure grinning fool. There was something there.

Would you-all mind leavin' me be, just this once?

Lester said We thought you might like a hand with that pony.

Thank you kindly. When I do I'll surely ask.

Finally they sauntered off. When they were out of sight the pony turned my way, circled round those reins on the ground, didn't step on them again. I figured one a them likely tried to ride him. At least fooled with him. Or maybe he watched one a them or some other cowboy try to ride some other pony, that had made an impression. I already knew around horses some things you can't undo, that seem to take forever to get past.

So I left him where he was, standing stock still behind those reins. Went into the barn with no idea what I was lookin' for, but found me some good green hay and two burlap bags that I stuffed full till the both of them added up to maybe a hundred-weight, then took some twine and tied their mouths together. When I went back into the corral I knew he could smell that fresh hay in those bags over my shoulder, and it had his attention. I angled toward him, then stopped a few paces off. Lowered the bags between us, and stepped away. He nosed forward and snuffed them a little, knew what they had to be but couldn't get at them. I took my time. Cooky came out on the porch and rang that big rusty truck rim they use for a bell, but we were too busy for breakfast. I caught up the reins and led him round the corral a couple more times, then came up alongside those bags like the rough pantslegs of a giant. Let him snuff around. Then I heisted the two bags into the saddle, let that weight settle on him, hang down either side. He turned his head, saw it balanced there. I clicked my tongue and we walked on around without a hitch.

I was set to tie those bags on if I had to, but he caught on right away. Wasn't bothered. We even took it around at a lope and they didn't fall off. Then I slowed to a stop, dropped the reins, pulled down the bags, bent over and untied one bag to dump out a flake or two. Let him eat some while I gathered the reins. When he'd had enough and lifted his head I spoke to him, just the kind of low steady nonsense horses love, then put a boot in the stirrup, swung up and set quiet. Watching one ear swivel, his head up watching and listening for me to click my tongue. Like he knew we had places to go, and was all set to take me there.

Dark Like the Lid Shut on Everything

Though they don't tell you that in the crib, you always do what you have to, and what you can, more or less. I signed on to the K-Bar as a kid on the run and never did double back to finish school or face the music. Figured I could read and write, lie about my age, steer clear of trouble and lay low. I thought for a cowboy that was plenty. I wore my innocence like a pair of creaky leather chaps, so the cholla of life couldn't stick me.

As for what we did on the place, the routine was simple: the boys drove the cattle up to the high meadows in spring, what we called the back country, then down again come fall. In-between the foreman would send a couple boys to ride up every other week and check on things. Except for spring and fall roundup, these were the only times we'd spend a few nights sleeping out. We'd heard several of the biggest ranches still had line shacks, gradually replaced by trailers parked up on blocks near where the shack roofs rotted through, but the Kendricks K-Bar had no roads, nothing but trails and proud of it, and a few tents and pack mules. When the nights were balmy and dry, which for most of the summer they'd be, the boys would build a fire to grill their burgers and beans and lay out their bags and blankets under the stars. On these rides we'd doctor any new calves and sick cattle we found, tag any strays, and catch a few wild ponies to train and add to our strings. It was as close to old-time cowhands as any nowadays got to be, and most watched what they said, so their days on a ride never came out sounding even vaguely like a complaint.

When I first signed on, the spread had a cowboy with only one name, Greaves, straight black hair, black eyes, solid and knotted as a pinion pine, serious as death warmed over. None of the hands ever saw his name spelled out, not even on an envelope, since he picked up his mail in town, care of General Delivery. He played his cards close to the vest, and why not. He was a top hand somewhere around forty, with his own way of doing things, thought out well in advance. The boss told him to do something, it was good as done. Never known to smile, though he was occasionally heard to crack a joke. The joke and his laugh both had that same sound, kind of a flat slap. And one more thing—Greaves was some kind of Indian. Mescalero, Kiowa, Commanche? Among the gringo cowhands, who's to say.

Greaves never had his horses shod, just trimmed their hooves with a big curved knife that he kept razor-sharp. No one ever saw him take a drink. And no one ever saw him break a horse. He'd rope a green pony and ride off on his own, leading it, and come back the next day set to work, with it eating out of his hand.

Which is all I knew about him till that early spring storm caught the two of us out riding the back country, just him and me. Apache wasn't along on this ride. He'd gotten an infection from stepping on some cactus spines, so I had to borrow a spare horse from Dwayne, another new hand on the place. It had been a long hard day tagging and doctoring, and we were bone-tired. After a bloody riot of a sunset we warmed some cans of stew, leaned back against our saddles and drifted off still chewing the last half a bite. Laid out on the ground in our bags. The next thing I knew I woke shivering under a snowdrift that had put out the fire. I called to Greaves and he sat right up. The wind was pretty fierce, so in short order we lit the coal oil lantern and packed up, untied our horses and mule, and worked our way on foot down off the mesa into a dense thicket on the canyon floor that gave a little shelter. There we got another fire going, not so easy this time even with some oil splashed out of the lantern, then set up the tent, and staked out the ponies and mule. The snow bounced its feeble light up from underfoot into a cotton-wool silence. It had snowed a foot and a half and was still bucketing down without a sound, bending the stunted trees over. We stuffed the coffeepot with snow, set it on to boil and shook out our soggy bedding. Though the temperature must have dropped sixty degrees and had us both shivering, we weren't in too bad a shape. We put on all the clothes we had, then our slickers. Greaves said nothing, just stepped off into the dark now and then to drag another dead tree in for the fire, that I kept wondering how he'd found.

The snow kept pelting down and piling up. The cold and silence deepened around us like a dam holding too much water, full to the lip. We were both wide awake, hunkered down in our slickers, poking the fire. Greaves seemed unconcerned with his comfort, not rattled by the dark, the swirling torn curtains of snow. Eventually we got sensible, tumbled the damp sleeping bags back into the tent and sat just inside the flaps out of the wind side by side, facing the night and the fire.

It might have been just the coffee made blind without the percolator, no counting the handfuls of grounds, or maybe it was the mounting snowdrifts that finally got to Greaves. In this dark like the lid shut on everything, something out of his past edged in close, and got him going. I asked how he got into the business working cows. He said What else, they shot the last buffalo. Then he blew out a long breath and started laying out his life like puzzle pieces dumped from a box, most face-down, a few face-up. Said he never met his father. Mother was a wild young girl who worked nights in a truck stop diner once her parents kicked her out and she moved off the Reservation. Not the wages of sin, but that old pregnant shame. She had a bunch of regulars, old diner loners who treated her like a daughter, tried to run off the wolves. They even babysat me once in a while, when they liked someone she was running with. I slept in the store room in a box of towels while she worked her shift. The only thing she ever said about my father was that he was a cowboy. When I was ten, come in late that first time, she said I was worthless as he was. I didn't bother to ask who she meant. It was the peach brandy talking. When I wondered what became of him, she said the state pen for armed robbery and car theft. Then she spit on the floor and fell straight back in bed. Nothin' more to be said. By then I'd already been to my first rodeo, seen the boys hang on, a few fan the air till the buzzer, so the damage was done.

Cowboyin' was the one chance I could ever see for myself. A lot of the tribe didn't think much of ranching and farming, but I started paying attention to every little thing around horses and cows. Found some places to hang out that had animals, as a kid will, and caught on pretty quick.

At sixteen I quit school, which was the legal limit, lit out and never looked back. I was twenty-three when the Kendricks K-Bar hired me to fill in for fall roundup. Did you ever meet Curley, or was he before your time? He was still laid up from that spill he took, when his horse fell on him, like to broke his back. Still drawing wages but took forever to mend, couldn't put on his own slippers, which sorry to say for a stray like me looked like hope. For a lot of us the bunkhouse might as well been home and family, least for those who owned not a thing but their saddle. We'd get hired and stick forever, for the bunk and three squares and the least little chance at a life that wasn't pure larceny. Sometimes this was just where a broken-down cowboy landed after he got thrown off a fancier place. If he was on the way down, like Curley, bent like a scrub pine windblown at timberline, bald as a boulder in a mountain stream, this was where he likely stuck.

Greaves went on and on. Told a tale on Curley bulldogging at the Pendleton Roundup for a blue ribbon that contradicted all he'd just said of that broken-down old man, that he had to be too young to have seen for himself. I'd never heard him like this. Hardly knew he could talk. Like a barn door blown open, all the ponies loose. He wasn't old enough to make me think he was dying. Or dead-tired from holding it all in. Or crazy, or plain scared. It might have been just the night for it, the snow and quiet that wouldn't quit, just kept getting deeper, soaked up and deadened all the little lives around, that might make you think you saw the end coming. Even as a kid I knew enough not to ask questions of a grown man. Like riding out a night storm on horseback, just give him his head, since he could see better than I could.

Then in the false dawn getting on toward sunup the weather turned. The snow lightened up then quit. A warm wind shifted around from the west. We settled back into our soggy covers and slept.

When we woke it was sunny mid-morning. There was still snow on the ground, especially in the shade and the north sides of hills, but it was melting. I could hear a creek roaring somewhere a little ways off. I gave the stock the few flakes of hay we had left in the tarp under the mule's diamond hitch. Then we stirred up the fire, made some fresh coffee and flapjacks in the frying pan. While we ate I studied Greaves out of the corner of my eye. Did he know how close to his story my own was? Did he regret running on and on?

He cleaned up his food without a sound but the fork scraping his tin plate, then he looked over and said Ben, let's go find us some ponies. Which startled me, since that was the first time he'd ever used my name. Then something else dawned on me, that hadn't before. Since he was a top hand and had his choice, he must have picked me for this ride.

We struck the tent and packed our soggy gear, then saddled up and set out. I hung onto the pack mule's lead rope and followed Greaves, since he was the one with ideas. We didn't climb back up to high ground, just followed the water downhill. In a few miles we came across some horses and cattle that had sheltered in the scrub like we had. We reined in at a distance on the far side of the creek and checked them over. We couldn't see any work to do on the cattle, no new calves, and all these ponies looked wild.

Greaves said There's one I've had my eye on, that black one with two stockings. I turned to look where he pointed, and nodded. It was a strong young filly with clean conformation, that showed good blood but plenty of that mustang stamina. With that wild instinct right away her head came up, and she looked back at us.
Think I'll cut that one out. You see one you like?
I still wasn't used to being consulted, but then took another look, and said What do you think of the gelding with the spotted face and neck?
He oughta make a fine one. Good strong hind end on him, got some quarter-horse.

Then Greaves pointed to the nearest trees, which told me to tie up the mule plain as day. I got down and took care of that, then climbed back aboard and shook out my lariat when I saw Greaves unlimbering his, easy little circles shaking out a loop.

Then one more look my way to see was I ready, and we were off. We eased though the swollen creek at a walk, then he surprised me by turning first toward my spotted one, cutting him out from the others without

bothering them much, heading him my way. I settled a loop over his head
and let my pony do his work, backed up to keep my line taut.

Take him back across and keep him by the mule. I'll see you in a little
while. I think that's what Greaves said, but he may have just pointed. But
that's what he meant, what I did.

Greaves headed on into the scrub thicket where the other horses had
vanished, and I tied my new pony to another tree where he couldn't get tangled up with the mule standing there minding his business, looking underfoot to find a little something to chew. I left my horse saddled just in case,
tied him to the same tree as the mule, and sat down with my back against
it, facing across the stream to the thicket that had swallowed Greaves up.

Three minutes later I was out cold. Then it could have been a minute or
a week, till something woke me. I peered out from under my hat and here
comes Greaves on that new black filly, with his horse right behind him,
with only a rope hackamore, running free. They look to be having a race,
and the filly is holding her own, even with saddle and rider. And one more
thing: Greaves looks to be soaking wet, head to toe. So is his saddle. And
what's more, he's got the strangest look on his face, like he's about to laugh.
Hey there, Ben. You set for some fun?

I must have looked hopeless, groggy as I was, but jumped up like I was
ready for anything. Greaves brought his horses to a halt without the slightest signal I could see, and sat there stroking the neck of his new mount,
talking to her softly, waiting for me.
What should I do with my new one?
Greaves said Bring him along, but cinch him up close so he stays out of
trouble.

And with that we headed off downstream, me bringing up the rear
with the pack mule and my new spotted horse, winding down the near
bank a couple miles until we came to a bend with a deep pool where the
water slowed. Greaves climbed down, loosened the girth and pulled off his

saddle and blanket from the black mare, rubbed her back while he talked to
her, then tied both his horses under a tree just uphill from the pool, which
they seemed to mind not at all.

Then he came back, caught the lead rope and tied up the pack mule
nearby. I climbed down off my horse, and stood holding my two ponies,
one in either hand, waiting to see what we'd do. He came back and took
my horse from me, led it away a few steps, loosened the girth and heaved
off the saddle and blanket. He tied another halter and slipped it on as he
unbridled the animal, smooth as magic, then led him to join the others.

When he came back he pulled a long scarf from around his neck, that
was still wet too. He wrung it out and handed it to me, said Stuff this in
your pocket a minute.
What's it for?
You'll see. First we have to saddle your new baby. With that he reached
in his pocket and pulled out a damp handful of rolled oats, that he must
have gotten out of the mess kit, and handed to me.
You get in front, use this to get his attention. Handle him all you can.
Hold him close and talk to him.
What should I talk about?
He just needs to hear your voice. You'll think of something.

So I got in front of that spotted horse, held my handful of oats out flat
under his nose, and started talking to him. Told him what I liked about
him. Greaves stood quiet till the pony was done snuffling and lipping the
oats, as I rattled on and on. I held his bridle close and patted his neck and
chest. Greaves picked up the saddle blanket and rubbed the horse's back
with it, then said Here, you do it, so I did.
Between us we bridled and saddled that pony, who was a little skittish
at first with the weight, then the girth, but eventually took it.
Then he had me lead the pony around on the bank, back and forth till
it didn't mind the saddle, and followed me, easy and trusting and alert.
When he was satisfied with how the pony behaved, he told me what to do.

You have to blindfold the pony with my scarf, tie it under his cheeks so he can't shake it off, then lead him into the water, which he won't balk at if he can't see. Stay to this side out of the current, but get him quickly to the deepest part of the pool. At the point where he's on tiptoe, starts to float and has to swim, you climb up in the saddle. Then take the blindfold off, and hang on. All the while, just pet his neck and talk to him.

Then what?

Just stay on. Keep him in deep water till he quits struggling, till he knows he can't throw you. If he does, just get back on. The smarter he is, usually the less time it takes. When he's done fighting it, you can bring him up out of the water and ride him around.

I stood there thinking it through. I looked uphill and noticed the black filly with the white stockings staring at us. And the other two horses, and the mule. All heads-up like statues. This is what he must have done with her.

So I tied on the blindfold, then clicked my tongue and led him straight into the water, which came as a shock to both of us, ice cold. He snorted and slowed but I just pulled him deeper in till he was floating, then climbed on. For a second or two he panicked, then I snatched off the blindfold. He couldn't duck his head to buck, was forced to swim with his head high so there was nothing else to do, and he knew it. All the while I kept talking to him, with my voice low and steady. Soon he was just swimming strong as you please, with my weight keeping him low in the water. When he was calm I turned him back around and offered him salvation, that sent him surging for shore.

On the long ride home, with enough miles so the ponies never minded swapping saddles, taking turns tasting the bit, getting used to it, Greaves told me that creek wouldn't have been deep enough to float the ponies without all that snowmelt. It's never that deep in the summer, there isn't a stock tank or pond deep enough on the whole place, without a serious rain. That warm weather in the morning woke me to the chance, thinking here come something like it was meant to be.

Somewhere along the way we named the new ponies Socks and Paint. And talked about how Indians used to ride and work horses a whole different way. By the time we rode into the big corral at sunrise next morning, tumbled back to earth and stood there shaking on our last legs, he didn't need to tell me not to say a word. As with every real teacher, here was a gift made to the cowhand and horseman he thought he saw in me, a blindfold promise made in hope, that might or might not see the light of day.

The Genuine Article

If I kicked off my boots, left the Stetson on a peg and put on a plain shirt and shoes to go to town, those days I could be anyone. I knew plenty of the boys would rather be caught fishing out of season than show up without their gear. The hat and boots, jeans and vest were a statement, an identity. They had let me hitchhike across the desert out to the coast, day and night, summer and winter, at a time when most just didn't do that anymore. Not unless they were in a full dress uniform, or broke and desperate to get to a funeral, they didn't care whose. Since that last one was my mother's, back in Fresno, I truly hadn't given enough of a damn, should have been more careful, but that time got by on my luck. But still and all, these days you might not be taken for a cowhand 'less you're sitting a horse. Set to touch your heels to his ribs and ride. To quell that talk of all hat and no cattle.

Because let's face it, some days even cowboys feel like the real thing is a thin disguise, a bowlegged daydream out of the past teetering along the edge of still making a living, jingling in the sun its rusty spurs.

So today here I was going to town, scrubbed and scraped and curried, in what might as well be a disguise, set to go up in front of a judge. And this was a judge that might have heard at least a little about me, enough to form an opinion as they say.

Once I got on as a cowhand at Kendricks' K-Bar there was a stretch that lasted out my twenties when I went to town every chance I got, which mostly meant Saturday nights. I didn't have a car or truck, and the nearest town had no more hitching posts, and out our way were shoulderless windy little roads not fit for man nor beast on foot. I could catch a ride with someone who had wheels, like my buddy Dwayne, or else walk. Then I would be stuck in some dark cinderblock den dug into a hillside like The Rustler's Corral, with a jukebox and Christmas lights, that smelled of stale beer and minty dipping tobacco, till my buddy felt like heading home. It could get hard if Dwayne got lucky with Angela, the sultry pale-skinned barmaid he had an eye on. Then I'd have to rustle me up another ride, or else make that eight-mile walk in the dark in my boots, with no coat or gloves on. But at least if one of the locals happened by while I was walking, they'd usually slow down, let me pile in the back with the chainsaw and stovewood.

Though I liked to drink a little beer and play some pool and shoot the breeze, those years any time I went to town I was still a little skitterish, used to laying low. Here we were a good two-three hundred miles out from San Angelo, but I was still on the lookout for anyone with a bad word to say to me from way back then, when my cousin Mayellen's husband Clyde Hooper laid into me with his belt that one time, and got what he had coming. Dumb seventeen-year-old kid or no, some things you don't forget, any more than a mistreated mule.

This trouble came one night when Dwayne and Angela had a serious falling out, argued to a tearful standstill out under the cottonwoods below the parking lot. She took off early and he lit out after her, both of 'em drinking and slamming and shouting. Then a couple hours later she called the Corral, and asked for me. Said Dwayne is too drunk to drive, she'd taken and hid his keys, and he'd kicked down her door and would have to pay for it. I said What do you want me to do, and she said Come get the fool and his truck. I said Where is Dwayne, and she said Passed out in the bed of his pickup. I put that old tarp over him. I told her Make sure he has air, and set off to walk to her place.

Her place was an old motor court from the fifties, out the far side of Farrington, that someone had added kitchens to, and front porches, and turned into rental units. It could have been a lot worse. And things were just like she said. Dwayne was laid out in the bed of his pickup gargling and snuffling like he'd had his throat cut. I got her to find me some tools, pulled the hinge pins and straightened out her door, put in some wood glue and a couple screws, and got it to square up and shut best I could. Then fired up Dwayne's truck and started the long drive home nice and slow.

But a few miles out the other side of town, up on my tail here come the flashing lights. The thing was, I didn't have a license. Never had had one, though my mom's cousin Mayellen had taught me how to drive when I was thirteen, since I was big for my age. Figured I would get the license once I'd saved up for the car. When the county deputy pulled me over, out on one of those dark windy stretches, I was pretty sober, three beers over four or five hours plus that nice long walk in the dark, but he was no older than I was, and wasn't about to see my side of things. It was Deputy Magruder, who knew me to see around town, and I knew him to nod to. I showed him Dwayne in the back, climbed up to fish out Dwayne's wallet and show him the registration on the truck, then laid out the truth of the matter. Which was that here I was stuck between a rock and a hard place, with a friend to get home, and not a soul to lend a hand. He wrote me a hefty ticket anyhow, $425, that would have bought a whole car with a bad battery and bald tires, but then let me drive on home before Dwayne could wake up and get in more trouble. Magruder said if there had been a service station open within a hundred miles he would have had the pickup towed, but that seemed like too much trouble for this late at night, with a body in the back and me only six miles from home.

Next Monday I got a ride into town with Bixler the Cooky on his errands, went to the courthouse to see about the ticket, and got a court date to tell my side to the judge. I figured it couldn't hurt, and maybe he would see his way clear to not throw the book at me. This was my first official run-in with the law, and I wasn't used to having to explain myself. Whenever the foreman would bawl me out for making a bonehead move, I'd just keep my head down and take it, say I was sorry and promise to never do that again, which was usually plenty.

But this court date couldn't help but get in my head. I turned it over and over, and tried to think what to say. Dwayne wanted to come along to stand up for me, testify if they'd let him, but I knew he'd show up in his cowboy rig which might not set so well, seeing as how the town folk mostly thought we ranch hands all rode on the wild side.

Sitting there in court waiting for my name to be called, I remembered one fellow who had picked me up when I was hitchhiking to my mother's funeral. He was a huge fat man, who said he was a cab driver, and had just got off work, pulled a double, two 12-hour shifts back to back. He stopped to buy us pie and coffee, then said Why don't you drive, I need to get me some rest. I just looked at him. He says What? I says You don't even know me. I could hit you on the head and dump you, and make off with your car. He just laughed. Said, How would you manage that? You couldn't even budge me. Besides, son, you don't steal things. You're a cowboy. Which I had to admit I was. Musta resembled the genuine article that time and no mistake.

Just then the bailiff called out Ben Wilder, and there I was up in front of Judge Norman Lacey. He looked me over a little, then said How do you plead?

Guilty, your honor.

For some reason he liked that, but seemed bothered by something else. Waving the officer's report, he said This says Driving Without a License.

Yes, your honor, that's me. But...

But what?

It was a special case.

Which is what, exactly?

I have a buddy broke up with his girl, and they got into it.

And?

I went to help him out. She called, said he wasn't fit to drive. So I walked over to her place from the Corral, and patched up the door he kicked in, and was just driving him home.

Which is where?

The Kendricks K-Bar out to the east.

You work there?

Yes, your honor.

You're a cowboy?

Yes, your honor. Only...

Only what?

I was gonna say, please don't hold it against me.

There was a roar of laughter from the court, and the Judge banged his gavel.

Mr. Wilder, we don't hold honest work against anyone.

That's good, your honor. This ticket's gonna more than clean me out.

The court has been known to make arrangements.

Yes, your honor. But if I had four hundred twenty-five dollars, I would already had me a car and a license. But then I might not a been in town to help him out.

How much do you have?

A hundred eighty-two until payday.

Is that still last Friday of the month?

Yessir. But how would you know that?

Mr. Wilder, This is my court. I'm the one gets to ask questions.

Yes, your honor.

Which reminds me, where's your gear?

Gear, sir?

You know. Hat and boots and the like.

I left that home today.

Why?

Thought it might prejudice the court. No offense, your honor. Figured to just say I had a job, so you might let me pay it off, and wouldn't jail me.

I have just one more question. How long you think it would take you to get a license?

A week or two depending.

Depending on what?

On when I could get an appointment. And the loan of a car. And if they'd let me take the time off.

I know how that is.

Yessir?

Happens I once worked out there myself.

The judge's remark got a hard burst of laughter from the court, which must have been in on the joke.

Is Len Dawes still the ramrod?

Yessir.

Well, you tell Len Dawes ol' Norman Lacey needs you to tend to this. Then you drop by here on the way home and show the bailiff your license. Think you can do that?

Yessir.

One more thing. I enjoyed that work much as anything I've done, and more than most. And wasn't half-bad if I do say. So there's one thing you might want to ask yourself, which is what I ask myself. Which is Why am I not still doing it? Did I get lucky, or did I get waylaid somehow, all turned around and lost, and never straightened out? Or did I just get so lazy and old and forgetful I could make out like it's not my fault?

He just looked at me, aimed his little wooden hammer and said Don't answer that.

Yessir.

Well then. Case dismissed.

And with that the judge banged his gavel, and over the commotion in the court, the bailiff shouted All rise. Then the judge stood up and walked out, wearing shiny black cowboy boots to match his robes. And going out I heard the bailiff say the judge wore a belt-buckle big as a skillet, considered a weapon by some in these parts.

Cowboy Love

Cowboy love was a pickle. Couldn't decide was it meant to be sweet or sour, songbird or screech owl with attitude loose on the night wind. Not to be trusted, since it had no place and no future. Girls told you that straight to your face even as they were two-stepping past you, twirling themselves like a lariat, flirting with capture a mile a minute. So at the very least approaching a girl was a zen arrangement in the now, one day at a time like they said at AA meetings in the church basement on squeaky folding chairs. Where you learned love was not for cowboys, where what you got in the long run was oily burnt coffee and stale cookies and the kind attention of strangers, after a drunken squeeze.

And that line the girls used about cleaning up nice, that seemed to have been invented for sunburnt weathered old boys who knew enough to scrub hard, rinse good and currycomb before they went to town in the blocked white Stetson and shined boots and brand-new fancy pearl snap-button shirt and Levi's with no holes, a getup that might cost a good two or three months' pay, yet to us worth every penny.

So I studied my buddy Dwayne a little warily these days, besot with his lovely new girl Angela, who waited tables at the Rustler's Corral a couple-three nights a week. She was going to community college, studying to be a medical technician, on track to be certified to run sonograms and other costly procedures. Like she said, it was nice to see for yourself what was going on, before they cut into you.

Angela was easy on the eyes, cheery, observant and razor-quick. Still, I couldn't help but feel what she had with Dwayne was just a fling before she moved on, landed in a big city hospital with young doctors on the make at every turn. Not that I blamed her for a minute. The romantic game was hard on women, and they did what they had to, to build a career, start a family, raise kids. And I thought I knew right where cowboys stood—outside the candy store looking in. I could even see why. Anybody who knew what I did, after four or five years in the saddle, about feeding, doctoring, pulling calves and whatnot, if he had a little savings or an ounce of credit would be buying land and a couple likely heifers to get started on a little spread. Which really meant social capital, family connections, that might let you cash in on the skills and horse sense that came along with being a cowhand.

So eventually you might grow up, wake up and fill out to be a rancher or farm equipment dealer or banker or a big-animal vet. Otherwise you might stay nothing much but a cowhand. You could give riding lessons, teach a clinic in barrel racing or calf roping, and a few in a hundred of you could for a little while hit the rodeo circuit until you broke something, and while you were mending wised up.

I know, here I go daydreaming off toward the big city and all it's got in store, that practically proves I'm in a rut with no future. Maybe what I need is to stretch my legs and go for a long ride, watch the sun come up and go down a few times, and snap out of it. I wouldn't have been thinking like this at all, giving the whole cowhand life a hard look, like swirling the kinks out of a lariat, if I hadn't just met a new girl myself. They will do that to you, won't they.

But it may have been just how quickly Dwayne took up with Angela, that really caught my eye. So even though they ran hot and cold off and on, Dwayne would not shut up about how quick and cute she was, bright as a new penny, how much just plain fun, till I had to go to town to meet her and see for myself. Which is exactly how I met Lena on a Friday night, parked there on the end barstool right at the heart of the action.

Lena was tall, slender, dark-eyed, dark-haired and fierce—and at first seemed serious about every little thing. Even when you didn't agree with her, her smile could be devastating, a searchlight that spun past you on around the room. A friend of Angela's from the community college, eighty miles away, they had met on the first day of an Intro to Biology class. They happened to sit next to each other, and since they both took pretty good notes, they'd quiz each other before every weekly test, right on up through the final. Their focus was interstellar. Nobody could touch their prep for thorough, and nobody else could break in on their study sessions, though plenty tried. For that whole semester they traded the top grade back and forth, and in the end tied on the final and got a matching pair of A's for the course.

And she was a pistol. Our first real talk was about whether horses were honest, what that meant. How you had to trust your horse and he or she had to trust you. Lena said What does it matter, providing you hold the reins, and there's a bit in their mouth? I said A lot of the time you're half asleep or minding something else, maybe roping a calf, so there has to be trust, otherwise you're just aboard a bomb, waiting for it to go off. A bomb, she echoed, and when I recited that cowboy conundrum, You want a horse to be bomb-proof, she choked back a laugh.

One problem I had with her right away—I couldn't get Lena to talk about herself. After the first couple times we met for a beer, I started thinking she must have this big secret she didn't care to spill. I had told her all about my father getting hit by a train and killed when I was 11, and my mom back out on her own in Fresno, still looking for love to blindside her any day. And how I'd gotten into working on ranches after running off at 17 from my cousin and her lunkhead of a husband who'd agreed to raise me. I didn't hog the spotlight either. I'd stop to take a breather, and ask her leading questions. But it was no dice. It got so bad I had to pull Angela off to one side and ask did Lena have something to hide, like a husband or a baby, or was I just doing it all wrong. She laughed in my face and said I think maybe she's a little scared of you. Just give her time, and rub her with liniment, and she'll likely come around. She likes you, that's clear enough. After all, you're one big strong ripsnorting cowboy, the kind most mothers around here warn their daughters about.

You think that might be it? Her family don't like cowboys?

What's not to like? Aside from your always being broke and off wandering miles from civilization, and what's worse, always off in your head, living like it's a hundred years ago where everything runs on firewood, hay and water, where it's all open range and no fences, and you don't mind if you smell like a horse and lay down in the dirt under a blanket and get snowed on.

I had to admit Angela had a point, so I tried to give Lena time and room. She might keep her secrets, but I was watching close, and there was no hiding how she laughed with her eyes. When something tickled her, those eyes would crinkle up in the corners, even when I could see her mouth trying to throttle back on a grin.

The Rustler's Corral was mostly where we met and hung out. It had an actual old corral below the place, down by Farrington Creek, shaded by cottonwoods. Word was the cowhands used to ride in from the range to the tavern, and turn their ponies out in the corral. But the back roads finally got graded and paved twenty years back, and these days there were almost never any horses here, except a few rare summer days, when several of the dude ranches would take all their city folks out for a ride, and set up a barbecue in the grove, with a bandstand and open-air refreshments on the side.

Twice that summer Dwayne and I took some time off, saddled our K-Bar ponies and borrowed some extras and spare saddles, and went camping with the girls up in the mountains where you could see forever and the nights were cool. It was mostly quiet and playful and grand. The girls seemed at home in the saddle, and the horses were part of our strings anyhow, so used to following along with no fuss. We had a campfire every night, cowboy cooking with a couple Dutch ovens and a grill, all of us well-fed, laying out under the stars gabbing away and listening to the night sounds all around. Near where we set up camp twenty miles from the nearest road was a waterfall with a pool one of the old-timers had told me about, and we went skinny-dipping there in the hot sun to cool off. We brought a bottle of tequila for toasting the sunset, but that was it for amusements, excepting Dwayne's harmonica that started when the talk dropped off.

I did all the cooking, just stepped up, planned it and did it, which had a surprising effect. Dwayne didn't know what to expect, since we'd only cooked for ourselves when we were riding the range, sleeping out three or four nights at a time, checking on the cattle. Otherwise I never touched a pan, and never told anyone on the K-Bar I'd had a cook job once upon a time. Angela started looking at me in a whole different way. And as for Lena, she ate like she was making up for years of starvation. And after dinners around the campfire she started to open up, tell about herself.

I don't know what I expected when it came. Turned out her real name was Helen, that she had changed in 9th grade. She was the only child of a physics professor who taught at a technical college, and a mother who worked in a book store near the school. They'd been happily married since day one, but had ways of smothering her with their love and expectations. She had rebelled, and been a real party girl through most of high school, couldn't say what had got into her, but barely graduated and wrecked two cars. Which kind of shocked Angela, who assumed she must have been studious, a hard worker and a leader. Lena said when she took that biology class where they met she just did what she saw the others doing—it was all monkey-see, monkey-do. I told her I didn't believe it. I had never met anybody as sharp as Lena. She said Chalk it up to motivation. I was ready for change, and could see I'd wasted every chance I'd had up to then.

A lot of the nights were spent by one couple or the other looking up at the sky for shooting stars. It was either that or watch one another in the heat of the moment across the campfire, by that flickering light. The sky offered meteors that flared and died down the wide sky, and watching their show seemed the least we could do by way of privacy, where there were no shades to pull, no doors to close.

On those two trips there was a lot of talk and laughter on the long rides out and back, and a lot of quiet time in the saddle, our little herd following and leading, being led. But then all at once fall arrived in the high country, and ready or not there was change in the air.

At the K-Bar one night over supper one of the old guys, Buddy Win-gate, seemed to have had it with the young guys being so noisy and cheer-ful, and decided to piddle on our parade. He finally said aloud what we'd been wondering, which was why all the girls seemed to show up at the Rustler's Corral. He said It's been that way since forever. You ever wonder what's the draw? It's all you innocent young roughnecks that have yet to get your hearts broke. The girls behave just the way you would, catching a filly to ride, hoping to find one that hasn't been messed with, not a quirk to her, not a scab on her, not a scar. The girls maybe feel like they deserve one innocent lonely real man in their life, just to see what that's like before they go getting serious.

I stopped Buddy, asked what getting serious meant, and he said Think about it. Bank accounts, loans and taxes, a real suit a clothes and a tie, a real job with benefits and disability, a retirement plan. And before you know it, baby bottles in the night and changing diapers. All that stuff you've heard but paid no mind, 'cause you're gonna live forever, on beans and biscuits and coffee, a wild thing all by itself way out on the open range.

As for getting serious, what can I say? It felt like Lena and I were in as deep as we could get. We'd gone off exploring together, and between the two of us did everything we could think of. It felt like she took me all apart, and put me all back together a whole different way every time. I don't know what I expected, but it got my attention, and seemed worth the work and the wait.

And then before I knew what happened it was done and gone. One more balmy night out under the stars making slow sweet love in the bed of Dwayne's loaner pickup. Then laying on the blankets with just our heads sticking out from under his tarp to keep off the chill and watch the old stars wander. Then all at once Lena gripped me tight, said she had something to tell me. And what she said was how we didn't fit in with her plans. Said she was off to see the world, and though she was too kind to spell it out, it was clear that didn't mean the far southern end of the K-Bar range where we were parked just then, but Houston, Chicago, New York, and who knew, maybe London, Rome, Paris and whatnot. She had enrolled in a regular college somewhere along the east coast, and wasn't holding out hope she'd be back out this way once her schooling was done.

Laying there next to her my heart raced in my chest like a wild thing in a corral, spinning and circling, trying to mount the bars and kick free. I couldn't breathe. I don't know as I had anything better planned for the two of us, had just been riding along as the vistas opened out ahead. The view was scrub cattle country, but still in all it was rich and various, wide and glorious, more beautiful and inviting than anything I'd ever seen on my own. But I had not a thing to compare it to, since she was my first, and now we were done.

It was like old Buddy Wingate had said, and I couldn't blame her, since her college would cost more in a year than I'd made so far my whole life. Which was maybe my education in what things were really worth. Or how you're taught to want what you can't get, then forced to settle for anything but.

In her sight that night I took it like a man, said goodbye and good luck, finished with a hug not a handshake so I could smell and feel her whole self one more time. But here was my life at an end. She'd packed up what mat-

tered and took it all with her. Back on the place I parked the truck, tucked
the keys under the mat and went off by myself. Next morning Dwayne
caught up my best pony Apache along with his own, came looking and
turned the pony loose to find me, which with his nose and hearing took
no time, and was not a bad sign. Dwayne fished some biscuits out of his
pockets and tossed them at me, which I caught on the fly. He knew what
had happened, and was too smart to say a thing but We got work to do, and
best be pushing on.

Trail Talk

Some thoughts come to you easier on the trail than in the bunkhouse, much less at a tavern the edge of town. Maybe a campfire just don't collect so much clutter as a barstool. Maybe it has to do with going where there are no roads, only sage and bunchgrass over rimrock, and the mud and dust of your going. Plus whatever time and work it takes to get up out of the rut of the ordinary.

One night the next summer out off the beaten trail past romance Dwayne and I were set to mend fence, and had ridden a long way through a whole lot of rough nothing to even get to where the work would commence. Along the trail to pass the time we'd started talking about rodeos and rodeo cowboys we'd known. Dwayne got to bragging on Bodacious, that killer bull that got retired so he wouldn't cripple up any more cowboys. He said he'd heard Bodacious hadn't been rode but a handful of times. Said he was too damn mean. In turn I told him about an article I'd read that said some bull owners who gave their horned demons clever names and campaigned them round the circuit made more money than all the cowboy winners put together. It seemed like the bulls were the real cash, the real story. We didn't rattle on nonstop. There were lapses and wind in the brush, cicadas and doves sprinkled through it. But as it sometimes will, the trail talk kept us at it, though by the end of the day the ponies were bone-tired as we were, and stood quiet on the line. We ate supper so fast in the dark we mighta spilled the beans but hardly missed a one, then sagged into our bags before we fell down. But we were still too wired from the long ride to drift off. Dwayne looked away at the stars awhile, then said Would you want to be famous, or what? I think he meant to ask more, like What would you give for it, and what would it change—but he stopped short.

To let him know I'd heard him I said Famous for what—sitting the best-looking horse? Sticking a bull for the eight count? But then went ahead and tossed in a few chips to fatten the pot. Said You mean since the Marlborough Man bit the dirt? When he still stayed quiet I said Seriously, I hope you mean famous for doing a little something, like a jockey winning races, making rich folks richer while he gets the dirty goggles. Depends was it for something lasting, that did folks any good. Like a new way to drill wells that never dug a dry hole. Or a cure for cancer, or for the pain I'm starting to get in my knuckles. But suppose I got offered fame and fortune on TV selling weed killer or lawn sprinklers—I'd have to say no thanks. But are you really talking about trading your shy little life for being dead famous? Maybe racked up like Evel Knievel, or dying some horrible death like those missionaries up in Canada two hundred years back, that the Indians tortured, sometimes killed for no more reason than to see how they liked dying, since they talked so much death and damnation, and the promise of eternal life.

Dwayne finally said I just wondered, does anybody with a lick of sense want to be famous, or would they settle for just being rich? And if getting rich is mostly a matter of luck, is plain luck enough, or has it got to be a hundred million worth? I've heard-tell of folks who one day said they just got tired being poor, so went and made a hay wagon of money, doing whatever paid best.

I said But then what do they do once the money shows up? I told him I thought this all might just be a white folks' dream of luck, to get so worked up by possible money that you could take one of those high-paying jobs that actually came your way, without craving to do the real work. But then I said Let's get down to cases. The whole thing about being a cowhand seemed to mostly be to do what you were told and take what they paid for it. Sometimes you had to cinch up tight and go without but didn't miss much of what you really didn't need. Because your horse still helped you each step of the way, and your buddies likewise, while you made do with what came, and learned to improvise. There were folks trying to teach people how to travel light, always carry a little bottle of dish soap and a piece of clothesline in their bag so they could wash their socks and underwear out in a bathroom sink and hang up. Not pack a thing but drip-dry, all set to go every morning.

I told him how I used to keep a can-opener in my saddle bags, then lost it somewhere so started opening cans with my pocket knife. Found it was one less thing to need, so wiggled that short blade around and never looked back. Which got Dwayne started on the notion of having a backup for everything, which made me think what else should a buddy be for, but to give you a light when your matches got wet, but I didn't say that aloud, because morning was gonna come early, and now that he was wound up, he might run long and loud as a river past a hard rain.

Still, it was a clear night out, the full sky turning easy in the wind without a sound, the ponies under the pale moon still as statues, so I laid there a while wondering what cowboy is deluded enough to love money much anyhow, that is only tolerable for the stuff it can buy that you can't make yourself. Money could get you halfway to a decent horse, providing you were in no hurry and knew what to look for, then gave him some attention and put in the work. But in the end money couldn't stop a good horse coming up lame, leaving you both afoot in the dark for the long hobble home.

Somehow we drifted off at last, then came the morning and work, that was a full-on bear all teeth and claws. We were here to replace a couple miles of the old barbed wire on the outer fence with four strands of smooth round heavy wire, but that damned rusty stuff still had a way of biting us, like it always bit the stock right through the leather, even when we thought we were done with it. We'd just as soon bury it in a hole out here but bundled it up to do the right thing, haul to the scrap metal place the next town over, the day after we got back.

The new stuff was 11 gauge, and came in coated 4000 foot rolls that were maybe 125 pounds apiece, that loaded down the four big mules we led, carrying two rolls each, tied on either side of their pack saddles, plus a sprinkling of hand tools. This stretch of fence went down across the floors of two canyons, up and over a steep spine between, Espinazo del Diablo. That Devil's Spine like to killed us both. So steep that everything we dropped slid or rolled a quarter mile.

Soon there were cattle all around curious to watch what we did, so we replaced the fence wires one at a time, top to bottom, so there was never a hole to slip through. And kept our ponies tethered close so we could give chase or run off the cattle if need be.

We were more than a week doing that job. It coulda been worse. In this
dry country, we didn't need to plant many new fence posts, as they were
slow to rot. By the end of the last day we were about as tuckered out as we
could be, had all we could do to toss our saddles off, feed and water the
stock. I had to make myself fry up some sausages, peppers and onions to
stir into the beans I'd had soaking, so we'd even make it through the night.
But by the time our plates were empty we were smiling back and forth,
thinking about where we were, with not a foot of good smooth wire left to
string and stretch.

Chewing away and mopping up, I thought of what we'd talked about
all the while we were building fence. Mostly we'd traded stories back and
forth about the horses and cattle we'd seen carved up and crippled by
barbed wire. Even a few cow hands. How barbed wire worked to turn and
stop animals, but when an animal got tangled up, stuck in a fence, it could
cost a life.

Then I said You remember what we talked about on the ride out and
that first night when we couldn't sleep, about fame and fortune? He said
Anymore I'm not sure, why don't you remind me. So I cut loose.

All week I'd been chewing on parts of that talk, not the money but
the fame. And far as I could see, fame just meant being known and talked
about in widening circles. For which there couldn't help but be jealousy
involved, since heaps of money might garner heaps of attention. Some old
Frenchman once said behind every great fortune there lies a great crime.
So folks are on the lookout for feet of clay, and the dirty ankles of anyone
dressed too neat and tidy. It might be okay to be generally known and
well-regarded, but not to the point of envy. You might be better off not being known on sight as a giver or taker, a healer or hard case, for skills that
might or might not prove helpful for anybody else. Okay to be recognized,
maybe called in on occasion for a helping hand, but mostly left to your own
devices. That let you pass unnoticed where you felt you didn't belong.

There I stopped. For a long minute we just looked at each other, then
started shaking our heads and laughing—and laughed till the tears came.
Fame and fortune? What was that even about? What did either of them
matter when you were faced with hard work that had to be done now and
done right? The fence work blew all that noisy talk away, like a rainstorm

erasing a drought. It was better that there be someone who'd hand you his fence pliers if you'd dropped yours, where they'd slid right off the mountain, and not waste a breath to curse the unfairness of life. While there was light to see, and steeples needed pounding, we always knew what was what. And from then on we'd occasionally introduce and point to each other as Dwayne and Ben, the Famous Fence-Stretcher Boys, that couldn't help but fetch a laugh.

Dingus

It had been a good hard ride, two days into the back country, an early
run trying out another source of income for the K-Bar, outfitting and guid-
ing a pack trip for some cheery Canadians. They were all one big farming
family from outside Saskatoon, celebrating the thirtieth wedding anniver-
sary of its patriarch and matriarch, with their children married and single,
including one young red-haired daughter who sang glorious sad songs with
her husband, in close harmony. It was all going fine until we had trouble
with one of the pack horses—Dingus. Of course he'd been trouble all
along, but then it came to a boil. We hadn't brought him to ride, because
he could be a handful. But the K-Bar was short of good horses that summer, for pack or saddle, and in exchange for the loan of the others, Len
Dawes told me to take him along and see could I make him behave. I was
trail boss, my first real chance to shine up front, and I hoped it wouldn't be
my last.

Maybe Dingus just wasn't cut right. That will happen sometimes with a
gelding. The horse still gets enough juice from his seeds to keep him randy,
make him half a stud horse, at least in his own mind. I hadn't worked
around him before, but could tell something was wrong. On the trail
Dingus was more than bossy—he'd try to take the lead no matter who was
riding point, or what his load might be. And he had a lot of quarter horse
to him, stocky and stout, so none of the boys wanted to tangle with him all
that much. Which meant he got used to having his way, which on a narrow
switchback trail or hogback ridge through high country could turn ugly,
should a horse put one foot wrong.

Nobody on the ranch knew exactly where that horse got the name.
Maybe it came from someone who had moved on, or started as a joke that
stuck. Nobody would own up to first calling him that as a colt, but we all
knew what it meant. It was the nickname Jesse James got during the Civil
War, when he rode with Quantrill's Raiders through Missouri, Arkansas

and East Texas. Some fool had named the horse after that murderous little renegade. Legend says the name either refers to an endless boast about his outsized member or else to a time when Jesse loading his revolver shot a chunk off his finger. Got so mad he was fit to be tied till he cooled down. And whatever Dingus meant, I have to say I've never known a cowboy to change the name of a horse, once that name got put to use, except to shorten it. Maybe it's like the superstition sailors have about never renaming a boat, stirring up doubt where you needed absolute trust. And here was a horse whose name might as well be a curse.

On this particular day we were crossing a high divide and going down into another watershed. But for most of the way there was no easy pass, no gateway and no notch. For the whole day we were riding a hogback ridge with a sharp dropoff on either side. A long ride with only a wide spot here and there, mostly nothing but rocks and thin air. No passing room and nowhere to turn around. And you know what cowboys say about horse sense. If horses were born with it, they'd rule the world.

I was riding Apache in the middle of the train, swiveling to keep an eye on both ends. The thing with Dingus was, he had to lead. Which I hadn't heard. The boys told me later they had mostly handled him by putting a big strong greenhorn aboard him and letting him go first. Which only served to make bad habits worse. Down on the level it didn't much matter. But on this trip with nobody riding him, he was just one of the string of pack animals tied together, strung out behind us. So he kept nipping at the heels of this big roan mare ahead, giving her the shoulder, trying to get around. Finally it got ugly, with the mare ducking her head and kicking at him, which worked loose and dropped half her pack load hundreds of feet down. We stopped right then, but with nowhere to pull up together or turn around we had to go on till we found a spot to rearrange ourselves. Nobody liked seeing that bundle go down the mountain, since at best it might be dinner, and at worst something we couldn't do without, like tents or toilet paper.

We talked back and forth a couple minutes, but there was nothing much to be done where we were. The younger Canadians looked a little uneasy, and who could blame them, since here we were up on the tin roof of heaven at the blazing height of day. But the silver-haired couple were calm. The nearest rider to the trouble was Bixler, our Cooky, leading the pack train with two animals ahead of Dingus, who was still fidgety, rearing and snorting. The one thought I had was to somehow put a drag on that damn horse, so I climbed down off Apache, handed the reins to the rider just ahead, took my lasso and worked my way back along the trail. I had to talk to each of the horses and hang off their stirrups to get around, or have each rider give me a hand, the trail in spots was that narrow. And dance a little with each horse, to see how they might let me by. I stopped for a moment with the mare, let out the line back to Dingus as far as I dared, then handled her a little and tried to calm her, but she was still stiff-legged and wild with fright. Then I dropped down the slope to one side, dug in my toes and swung past Dingus while he stood there staring at me. When I was beyond him, I dropped a loop over his pack frame and pulled back over the next horse's pack, to keep some tension on him. Then I gave the word to take it slow, and stop at the next spot we could.

That couple miles were pure hell, with me on foot, digging in my heels and getting dragged along, with that mare still kicking at Dingus whenever he got close. I kept my line tight enough to keep him from surging up and crowding her off the trail. But that mare still had her ears laid back, and was rolling her eyes. When we finally got to a wide spot and pulled up at a little saddle between two peaks, we were all exhausted. I pushed my way up to Apache and pulled my saddle off him, then lugged it back down the line, pulled the pack and frame off of Dingus, threw my saddle on him and cinched it down. Bixler helped me make the switch, and at one point he leaned close and said he had an old .44 Bulldog in his saddlebag, and I was welcome to shoot the son of a bitch before he took us all to perdition. I hated to put that pack frame and load on Apache, since he was the best cow horse the K-Bar had ever seen, but knew he'd be fine and do what he was told. I planned to bring up the rear and ride Dingus myself. I couldn't think of any other way we'd make it down off this hogback without further loss. I asked for a volunteer to go back and see could he retrieve any of the mare's lost load. Dwayne stepped up and said he'd do it. I gave him my rope and one of the other boys lent him another, which with his own just might reach down from the trail.

Then we formed a line and set out. The sooner we were down off this high rough ground the better. No one was enjoying the view, which was spectacular, and the only reason to come up here. Everybody was rattled, needed a meal and a rest. I held Dingus way back, behind the pack train, and didn't give him his head for a heartbeat. I had plenty of time to study him. He was strong, sure-footed and alert, with an easy motion and the makings of a good horse. But he never relaxed, and was a hog for attention, focused on something off in his own head. Somewhere something had gone wrong. Maybe he had never bonded with a rider, or had been starved and ignored. Something in him always seemed to be laying in wait, plotting mayhem. These were the earmarks of a tortured animal. Somehow Dingus had become convinced the enemy was other horses, and he acted like a stallion around mares in heat.

Sure he was fearless, strong and quick, but that pushing and crowding other horses, and fighting with his rider made him more than a handful, made him dangerous. Nobody would ride a horse like that for fun, only for the occasional wild rush, like General Grant after he broke the siege at Vicksburg. Dingus might never take to the work of herding cows. A cowboy would only bother with him if he did something no other horse could do.

We kept going till the shadows got long and the light began to fail, but were back down in the valley by sunset, and set up camp in the twilight. I unsaddled and tied Dingus off by himself to a stout juniper, looked him over and handled him, gave him a little attention and a kindly talking-to. Then on the far side of the clearing, I did the same for Apache. We all settled in for the night while Bixler got the coals going, and whipped up a dinner of steaks, potatoes and beans. Dwayne staggered in just after dark with most of the mare's gear we had dropped, including toilet paper that had already been missed. And a lucky bottle of rye whiskey that I cracked open and passed around to pour in the coffee, where no one begrudged its effects.

Around the fire that night the talk was better than expected. Hardly a thing by way of complaint. It felt like this kind of thing was what they had come for, expecting us to somehow do the impossible, in a wild lonesome setting, and make it look easy. Somebody asked me what I told that mare on the trail. I said Just the kind of lies and nonsense horses love, that I was going to keep him off her if I could. Which gave them all a laugh. Bixler said Why didn't you shoot him when you had the chance? I said I would have, but it weren't my horse. Besides, it mighta been a waste of good horse-flesh. At least a good bullet. And I was already so tired I'da never gotten my saddle out from under him. For a while the laughter just kept coming, like sparks swirling up from the fire, lost overhead in the stars. Then I lay back, and drifted off to someone playing a ukulele, and two voices singing The Streets of Laredo, in perfect harmony—two lovers so closely attuned they breathed as one.

When we got back home the foreman Len Dawes and I had a little talk. He asked me pretty much the same things as the Canadians had, but by then I had been riding Dingus for three days, had him eating out of my hand, as the boys liked to say, and had had another thought. I told him I wasn't sure Dingus would ever make a fair cow horse, though with a strong hand he just might. But he had such a good jump and speed to him he might make the perfect racing quarter horse. It's for sure he can't stand nobody running out ahead of him. At least you could try him later in the year at the county fairs, with a light rider, and if he does all right, that's what you could sell him for. Meanwhile, he's got that name everybody remembers, so there's no false advertising.

In the end he worked out fine, won races for a couple years. Then the price of beef picked up, so we got out of the packing horse business. And seeing as how he was getting famous, one of the boys finally took to him, and got him working cattle, so we kept the damn horse around, both him and his dangerous name.

Back-Country Justice

With cowboys you never know till you do. And this was a classic case of what some kids used to call Finders-Keepers-Losers-Weepers. But then we were no kids. For the time being I had taken to squandering my spare days riding the back country, sussing out vague little game trails in some of the wildest mountains in these parts. I can't say as I was looking for much of anything on these rides over the slow summer season, that might go on a week or two. One or another of the boys would come along for the ride and fresh air, since they were in roughly the same predicament.

What I was really doing before I even knew it, was scouting the Escalera Wilderness, what the boys called the Old Stairsteps, thinking to see could I maybe guide some pack trips up in there, figure out what the camping, fishing and hunting were like, see could I bushwhack a way through the maps and trails and rules, maybe make a go of it. Guess I was looking to replace something I couldn't seem to find, call it a little romance, with some old-fashioned adventure. And with the ranch business in a deep dip, and us on the verge of a layoff, maybe it was a way of plain marking time while mostly kidding myself.

So on the longest trip of that summer Dwayne and I were camped along this ridge looking down into a deep narrow canyon that widened and emptied out to the southwest, a far corner of some truly wild and desolate country, back in thirty or forty miles from the nearest gravel road. I was up before dawn to see where the deer might be feeding, scouting hunting prospects with a borrowed pair of binoculars. Sure enough, I found some does up early too, grazing the far side of the canyon maybe a mile off while their buck must have been hiding somewhere back in the trees. Then as I eased along the rim, looking for that buck above the does, I caught a flash of yellow in among the trees, that only showed from one point, along one side of a wind-swept old juniper where I'd plunked myself down for a look. A step to either side and the yellow was gone like a trick of the light, that you only wondered if you saw, that you might never spot from the saddle, with nowhere on this trail to stop or turn around. A speck of garbage maybe, the one thing for forty miles around that for sure didn't belong.

I looked around for some landmarks, and lined it up with a deadfall high on the rim opposite. I only hoped I could find this big juniper again from the far side, with its frayed and battered top torn open by some storm.

When I got back to camp, I stirred up the fire, put on the coffeepot, and looked after the horses while Dwayne roused himself. We'd been out for twelve days and were down to a few pounds of oats and maybe half a bale of hay. I checked along the line to see what they'd been eating, hoping they were finding something to go on. I gave each horse a big handful of oats in a nose-bag, then a flake of hay and called it good as they'd likely get till we stumbled down out of this country. My Apache got a little more, and a rub along the neck and a scratch around the ears because he's mine.

With the eating done, canned hash, onions and beans, we cleaned up and broke camp. It was about time to double back and head for home, which is always a bittersweet moment, as predictable patterns of work beckon and the chance to roam free has to end. We'd been scouting a place to cross to the far side of this canyon, since the way here was a serious climb up a tilted rock stairstep jumble. The far side couldn't be harder, and might even turn out easier. Besides, nobody liked being forced to walk backwards, retracing his steps the whole way.

Without being told, the horses knew we were heading home, though they might also sense that it was still a long ways. But in spite of short rations they were cheery and alert. By noon we'd found a way through the waggling damp split at the head of the canyon, and were scouting the far side for a way down when I thought to look for that big headless juniper from this morning, on what was now the near rim. We needed to rest the animals anyhow, so we strung them out along a line, and I started looking for the headless tree and that flash of yellow I'd seen. Dwayne wondered what I was up to, but I couldn't rightly say what it was, even to myself. Just something out of place in all this busy emptiness.

Turned out we couldn't see a thing from above, so I climbed down to the clearing where I'd watched the deer, and edged along toward the trees. I was practically past it when I looked back across the canyon to line myself up, then turned left into the hill and there it was. Two yellow wedges folded together under the dry evergreen canopy, sheared off and scissored by two trees that held it stuck. What looked to be a little yellow high-wing single-engine plane, folded like a sleepy grasshopper. The scrub trees were so dense we had to fight our way in. The plane was nose-down, the windshield gone, the oversized wheels of the landing gear torn away, and there were two bodies—two men slumped against their safety harnesses, hanging shriveled, dark and leathery in frayed and faded clothes, so long gone they hardly smelled of a thing but pine and juniper. Two men that could have been carved out of walnut, hardly a mark on either one, though both heads might have hit the windshield. They hadn't been eaten by animals, though the more we looked the more they seem to have been nibbled round the edges. The inside of the plane was packed half-full of pine needles. The blades of its prop had bit dirt, and were curled back like the last silver petals of a tulip gone to glory.

I tore open one of the doors, went through their pockets, pulled out their wallets and found papers in the glove box, that gave us registration numbers and ownership for the plane. The one I took to be the pilot had a massive gold Rolex watch on his wrist that was stopped but otherwise intact, and the passenger had two gold chains around his neck, one with a miniature gold safety razor blade. Dwayne was dubious, ready to leave it all and walk away until I dug into the cargo space behind the seats, and under the pine needles found a large duffel bag full of cash. Forty or fifty pounds, a couple bushels' worth. Old worn bills neatly bundled with paper wrappers for easy counting. I poked around through the needles but there was nothing else but handfuls of the windshield's safety crystals, a flashlight and some flares.

Later that night, after eating our beans up on the ridge around the fire we counted the money, that amounted to $723,000 and a few odd loose bills, plus a couple hundred each from the wallets of Juan Ramon Hernandez and Wesley B. Stokes. We both sat quiet a little over that. This plane with its fat tires and tailskid could have landed anywhere, on either side of the border, and taken off practically straight up from a donkey track.

Finally Dwayne dug around in the cooking kit and treated each of our tin cups to a splash of whiskey, then got to the heart of the matter.

What do you think happened to these two?

I think they were looking to buy or sell something. I think they'd made their deal and were on the way home, but maybe not. I think they flew up this canyon at night or in low light, didn't see how steep and tight it was up here till it was too late. They couldn't climb out or turn around. Just plain run out of room.

What do you reckon we should do?

I don't rightly know. Let's think. We've been off our last Geodetic Survey Map a couple days, so I couldn't even say exactly where this is, though I could bring 'em right back here, or close enough.

Bring who?

I don't know. Border Patrol, I expect, Immigration. Maybe just Sheriff Barnes or a couple of his strong young deputies.

But good God, Ben, will you look at that money.

What's your point?

We could just keep it, never say a word.

And do what?

I don't know. Maybe live a little.

Your Angela would like that, wouldn't she.

That's not fair. Sure she would. And I won't lie, I'd like it too. Tell you the truth, Ben, so would you.

I couldn't do it.

Yes, you could.

I wouldn't.

Why not?

I can't live like that. Neither can you.

Why? What's wrong with it? It's not like we're stealing. They're dead. Don't matter to them either way. And it looks like a private operation. That pilot Stokes is the one that owned the plane.

It's not about them. It's about us—or me anyway.

Dwayne found a scrap of paper and leaned close to the fire, worked out the numbers with a pencil against his saddle bag.

I make it out to be $361,723 apiece. Not bad, and not really all that much.

He sat there looking over at me. Said You know, if those Immigration and Border people stumbled onto this, they'd split it up, stuff it in their pockets in a heartbeat. And don't start with me on those deputies.

Dwayne, this ain't free doughnuts and coffee.

No, it's the cost of a decent little spread.

Look. If we can find this plane, somebody else is bound to. It's just a matter of time.

So?

So you turn up in town and buy you a piece of land with cash, that amounts to more than you could make in a hundred years as a cow hand. Can you imagine how hard they'd look at you?

Yeah, but there's nothing to find.

So you say. They'll just follow the back trail, like they do with dope dealers, corporate criminals and the like. Pretty soon they'll have you chained to the desk in some back room past midnight of the second day, asking you what you did up in the mountains last summer.

We could tell 'em the truth, just leave out the money part.

And how would that look?

Like what it is. Two guys died in a plane crash.

That they wouldn't be looking for, unless they'd crossed the border illegally. Unless there was a ton of the green missing somewhere.

Okay. Okay. Don't look at me like that. So what do you think we oughta do?

Head on home in the morning, with the money and papers and wallets and gold trinkets and all zipped up in that bag. I only wish we had a camera. When we get there we should take it in to Judge Norman Lacey, set it on his desk, and tell him what we found. He's a county circuit judge, he'll know just what to do. Let him figure out who to tell what and when. If any turns out to be ours, I'm betting he'll see it gets back to us.

You sure, Ben?

I'm sure. But first, I think we should finish what's left a that bottle.

If you say so.

With that, Dwayne dug out the whiskey, and topped up our cups.

Then he looked down into his, swirled it around and said Do the right thing—but how come it's so hard?

It's not hard, we just don't like it. But then again we don't have to.

Then why do it?

I don't know. I don't take stuff that's not mine. That's not who I am.

We're not bandits, we're cowboys.

So four days later that's just what we did. Dropped the bag on the man's desk. Wrote out and signed statements. More than a year after that we got a finder's fee, kind of a reward from the state, of ten percent, that we split down the middle. That Dwayne said was better than a pointy stick in the rumpus. We never heard if anybody rode all the way back in there and buried those two men. They woulda still been plenty hard to find.

Blindered Ambition

Long in the tooth, most of the old boys were well past blindered ambition, with its delusional weather. They rode, sat and worked their ponies with their hats pulled down, their chins tucked, just looked out ahead for sure sign—sunset and sunrise, payday, storm clouds and rain bearing down. They had some fun, sure, cut loose at local rodeos and fairs, even got a little worked up over the spring and fall cattle drives, where any fool could see how well or poorly the K-Bar was faring, if their job was safe. All anyone had to do was count cows.

But here on the place we were hired hands, all we'd ever be. Tethered to a warm dry bunk and three meals a day, with something to do that called for a certain skill and attention, that always took longer than need be, which by turns made you sweat and shiver. So much stuff to keep an eye on just ahead, we might as well have been wearing blinders, like harnessed beer-wagon Clydesdales. Ambition on the other hand meant a little something all your own, a piece of land where you might graze a few decent breeding stock, likely build a herd, also keep a little love you might not quite deserve but could learn to count on and treat right, a couple matching rockers on the porch of an evening, sip a cool cup of never-mind. Which mostly meant you had to take it all on your shoulders, keep your head, and weather the blows as they come.

There would always be a couple of the younger hands who craved to make it onto the rodeo circuit, who if they did well enough locally at the big events like bull riding, bronc riding, bulldogging, whatnot, would eventually talk themselves into taking a season off to go chase the dream. When they left we'd wish them well, and mean it, if they weren't too full of themselves. But then most would come limping back, grumbling over the luck of the draw, not getting the breaks, missing the buzzer by half a heartbeat. There would always be something to blame, when the fact of the matter was what they were doing was hard, even with nobody watching, even without the big clock and long odds stacked against them, with too many broke-down old cowboys perched on the top rail like buzzards, putting the hex on 'em.

I never did chase that dream myself. Could be I lacked the stomach, maybe not enough of a showoff, just too serious and methodical. Wanting it right the first time, no sense treating work like a game. Or maybe it was just having come from the wrong side of the tracks, with never a spare nickel, where there was no one with the patience to patch me should I hurt myself. I'd seen enough hands laid out by horses and cattle, that should have been watching and weren't.

Back then I had already started saving for my own place anyhow. I had lost my first love over what looked to be her ambition, her need for a wider world than I was offering. Maybe for Lena I was just a summer fling. At the time I had thought all life held was a nest, a little feed and shelter, and the sweet stuff we shared might just about cover the rest. So I kept saving for a likely piece of ground that might draw another cute moth to the flame. I knew there was no way to get rich overnight. I had bought a lottery ticket exactly once, while one of my buddies was buying one on a payday at the Rustler's Corral. Avery turns to me and says Hell, Ben, you know somebody's gotta win, might as well be me. And if not me, why not my buddy here? So I slapped down my money, regretted it in a heartbeat, knew there went a few bucks I'd never taste the good of. So go ahead, call me a loser.

Then for a long while no girl I took an interest in ever let me close enough, so the dream kinda faded in the wash, while the bank account never got within range of a fair patch of dirt. The price of land kept creeping up just out of reach. Maybe it was me doing the fading, that couldn't think up a good enough plan. But from then on I kept working for wages, banking my pay by the month, trying to wise up and keep my fool head down.

One night along in there Dwayne was telling me how his daddy liked big horses, till one threw him a mile and left him to hobble home on a crutch he whittled out of a tree branch. Said after that he'd settle for one small enough to wrestle to the ground. But then Dwayne said it's in the nature of humans to want to ride something bigger and faster than they are, which is what horse racing is still about. Without a horse the jockey is a fearless wiry little nothing wearing shiny silk britches. But up in the saddle he knows to hang on like a tick, rein in the big thing till the far turn then turn it loose with incentive to run like the wind. Probably that's what keeps us working for any big outfit—corporation, government, whatnot, army, navy, marines. Something so big it's practically indestructible, that makes us feel important, like without little me it could hardly wake up much less run.

Which I must admit feels like the K-Bar some days. Not that I could do it without a good pony to keep the cows in line and outsmart 'em. And eight or a dozen good hands to keep up with me. But where we sometimes drive a thousand cows in the fall of a good year, with just the handful of us to head and turn and keep them moving, spread thin as we are, can make for ticklish business, that when we pull it off can't help but feel like we got something done. When we swing the gate shut on the last of them, haven't lost or damaged a one, that amounts to something more lively than wages. The owner and the foreman know what it calls for, a cold beer and a barbe-cue and a couple fiddle tunes.

I was thirty-one when things took another turn, got more serious. I quit talking to real estate brokers, and started poking around on my own, asking hard after small places that must be hid somewhere. I had heard oldtimers in the bunkhouse talk about how some retired folks who hadn't saved enough might be willing to work out a deal. So I went to the county courthouse in Farrington, started looking through the records for places of a size I might afford. Then on my Sundays off I'd put gas in Dwayne's pickup and go driving the back roads, pulling in here and there. I had my eye out for a place that needed work, a little rundown and rough around the edges, that could use a hand, a place that some folks might sell me for a steady income to live on. Since I had room and board at the K-Bar I could let them stay there, long as it would be coming to me when they were done.

Then all at once here it was. Down outside Amity, sixty-eight miles from the K-Bar as the crow flies, I turned into a barnyard and pulled up. A bluetick hound crawled out from under the porch to sniff at me, but only bayed a time or two, then lost interest. While I waited by the truck this old couple stepped out onto the porch, blinking in the sunlight. The woman had her long silver hair in a bun, and wore a faded blue apron that matched her eyes, that she was wiping her hands on. She called out Rider, the dog came to her, and she petted him. He circled the boards in the shade and eased himself down. The old man was tall and spare, had boots and jeans and the right kind of hat on, a battered dirt-brown square-brim thing that might have once been black or white, that had seen all manner of weather, that had shaped itself to his head, that would take a tornado to lift.

I stepped close, snatched off my own hat and introduced myself. Said where I worked and all, that I was a cowhand. Delicately stated my business, such as it might be. That over time I was looking to build a little place, but was gonna need help on account of my ignorance. I was scouting a place to buy, hoping someone might be in no hurry to get all their money.

At that they both laughed a little. Wes and Gerty Birdsall were their names. This was their place. But then the first thing he said was Did I see a for-sale sign out along that road? I said Please forgive my presumption, I meant no disrespect. But before either of us could say another word, Gerty said This is no way to treat visitors, standing around in the hot sun. Come on in for refreshments. Which we did. I followed Wes through the house, that smelled heavenly, some kinda spice in the air, out the kitchen door onto the back porch, where there was a dishpan he pumped full from the cistern, a bar of brown soap in a saucer, and a towel hanging on a nail. We washed our hands and dried off, then went back into the kitchen and sat down. There sitting cooling on a wire rack was a fresh pie that must have just come from the oven. The place was warm but tolerable, and there was coffee percolating on the wood stove, in a blue enamel pot that wore a lifetime of soot.

I'd been trying to figure how to get around to the hard parts, but realized there might be no easy way. Then it tumbled out like a topping all over Gerty's peach pie. We ate pie and ice cream, seconds and thirds till it was gone, then looked around at each other and laughed. I said I usually never have seconds on dessert, and Wes said Neither do we. But we musta needed that. By then the hardest parts had been touched on, life and death and money, so mostly what we had was the small easy stuff from then on.

I learned a lot. Within minutes I gathered they'd lived here since Wes got out of the army in 1946, built the place from scratch with his two hands—and Gerty's, since it turned out she'd been a riveter in Pasadena at a defense plant. Wes and Gerty had always wanted kids but could never

have any, and had no close family left. Wes had worked as a cowboy on
a spread an hour south of here, till he had a horse lose its footing and roll
over him coming down off Haystack Mountain. Broke his pelvis, laid him
up half a year. Which got the two of them thinking out what they had of a
future. The Birdsalls had just shy of two hundred acres, a pole barn, maybe
twenty acres that had been cleared and planted but not for the last several
years, a lush little garden patch and all the rest scrub pasture and hills. One
nice little pond that had fish in it, and a decent well drilled deeper than
they had any right to expect. They'd had horses until a few years back,
when they'd found good homes and sold them off. Now they were thinking they mighta been a bit hasty, missing the animals that gave them a little
something to tend to, dream on and consult.

After a month of visits we had papers drawn up and signed. My savings
and ten years of payments and the place would be mine. Then they had me
out for chicken and dumplings and another peach pie that we laughed over
right from the start, and polished off every crumb. Gerty said I don't make
dessert but once a week, so really all it is, you're saving us from ourselves.
I said I don't buy that for a minute. On that visit Rider finally come up
and licked my hand, that we took as a sign. So I started paying them, but
mostly nothing changed. I bought a couple promising young mares off the
K-Bar, that Avery and Dwayne helped me breed to the best stallion on the
place, that when I went to pay for, Len Dawes called one of the perks and
waved me off.

At first I spent every minute out with them I wasn't working, mending fence, hauling scrap, cutting firewood and whatnot. I was careful to
seem in no hurry to get to the bottom of anything, but talking with the
Birdsalls while working alongside, pretty soon I got to hear about all their
comings and goings. How they'd met at a box supper social at the Method-
ist church in Pasadena, where Gerty had put a whole banana cream pie in
the box, that they ate before they even dug down to her fried chicken and
potato salad. And the dreams they'd had for their place, over the years the
different notions they'd tried. Had a run at raising turkeys, but it was too
far to market, the coyotes were bold as brass, and the big birds too pathetic.
At one point desperate for money Wes and Gerty had taken a turn being

caretakers for some well-to-do people with a big show place further south. They'd answered an ad in the paper. Turned out these were movie people, with more money than brains, that craved to be waited on hand and foot. Half of every week they'd spend running to and from airports. That had eaten up six months, before they shook loose and got back to their lives.

We had some good years there, Wes and Gerty and me. Wes had a crust on him but they were awful kind, and most of the time seems like they practically adopted me. Which to look back on it now must have been about what I needed though no way did I deserve. They never quit saying I should find a woman of my own to hook up with, and never gave up hope. At one point early on I built another room onto the house so I could come stay for the weekend, Saturday afternoon to Monday morning, which got to be our routine. I'd have a project to work on, and there'd be those two mares and their foals that I'd patched the fence for and moved in, that gave us all a little something to cheer on. If you give a damn about horses, there's nothing like having one of your own right from the start, where, if they don't turn out right, you got no one to blame. And Peaches and Hank turned out to be a rare couple dreamboats.

But then, as we all knew had to happen but not when, one day things took a turn. Getting down from the hay loft Wes fell off the ladder, landed on a couple bales. Which could have been worse, but was bad enough. Cussed himself, called it kid stuff, but had a hip and shoulder that had to get pinned, and were slow to mend. Gerty could still cook up a storm, but couldn't handle lifting and moving him. So they let me take five weeks off the K-Bar, and help out till he was on the mend. For me it was a great time, let me pay back their kindness a little, though I could see the time weighed heavy on both of them, that they couldn't help but see as a taste of what was to come. But Wes bounced back, with a little more hitch to his gid-dyup. He vowed to watch his step, although no one was reckless enough to mention that. I'd built a ramp down off the front porch, which appeared to depress them too, that made us all think of watching our step.

The day Wes had his final checkup from his big city doc, I begged off, said I had work and let Gerty drive him in. Then threw a surprise party for them that included every person any of us knew. I tied a huge bouquet of balloons to the mailbox out by the road, and slapped up a sign painted on a 4 by 8 sheet of plywood that said Birdsall Party. I invited folks from the grocery where they shopped, and some from their church, and their docs and nurses and receptionists. Even asked Bonnie, their favorite teller from the bank. I invited everyone off the K-Bar too, got the boys to help me carry tables and chairs out to the open yard, got a barbecue going and a tub of ice with cold drinks and melons, and set up their old hand-crank ice-cream maker that couldn't help but give us all a good workout, and make for something special.

Most of the boys had never been out to see the place, and were properly impressed. I could see some hiding their envy, while studying how me and the Birdsalls seemed to work things out. I knew a few of them looked to inherit a little land from families that I'd never had, and a few were running away from a family business that would have taken them in. But I could see around the fire in the yard after sundown how this kind of place might look more or less like home. Len Dawes and even ol' Lionel Kendricks himself drove out together, and ate and drank and chatted up the Birdsalls like visiting royalty, even had some of Gerty's by now famous pie, that for sure tickled her.

I learned that day how for folks like them getting on in years, you take the good days as they come. And even then take a sip at a time, don't let your feelings get to moving like a cow pony so quick they run out from under you. At dinner when everyone had them a plate, Wes heaved himself up from his armchair and proposed a toast, with a longneck beer in his hand. He said Here's to hay in the mow and the manger, here's to rain on the roof in the winter, here's to keepin' the dirt off your neck while you can. At that those cowboys purely whooped and hollered, while he took a little swallow, turned around slow as his old dog Rider, give everyone a wave, and sat down.

That next spring I borrowed a neighbor's tractor and plowed all the land that wasn't in pasture, planted clover and timothy, put in a little orchard of fruit trees near the house that we could water from the cistern, and started eyeing clouds passing over like I never had before. This is dry country, with plenty of dark cloudy looks, rumbling false starts, empty threats and promises. When rain arrives it can be an event. If we've had to wait half a year, we may be forgiven for dancing in mud puddles, snatching off our hats to let it beat our brainpans silly, hoping it keeps up till the ground is soaked and the hills green up again. I was only holding out for ten acres of hay, that woulda fed our four horses and then some. But it was not to be. That first year was a drought that by mid-July had already burned up practically everything. The Birdsalls watered the garden after dark, and we strung up some netting to keep off the birds, though I couldn't much blame 'em. There just wasn't a thing to eat out in the hills. Even on the K-Bar we had to feed a little hay through the worst of it, come August and September.

Wes's fall had aggravated the old damage to his pelvis, so now he needed a cane to get around. He got more and more frail, but kept his spirits up, tried to keep a step ahead and never let the lumps and hitches show. When he got out of bed in the morning, he already had half a dozen things figured out for the day, though little by little those turned out to be sayings not doings. For a proud quiet man like him it meant he turned into a belated talker, which was fine with me. It got easier to pry stuff out of him. In the first years he'd have crooked a finger at me and stomped off to the workbench in the barn to show how a thing needed doing. Now he'd have explained it twice, with tales and embellishments, before we got within smelling distance of the pile of manure to be spread.

For a while this talking phase gave Wes an unexpected lift. Though he was slow launching himself, he couldn't wait to get up and greet the day. Though the body was stiff the spirit was willing—he found he could talk his way through practically anything, especially if I was coming by, to do the heavy lifting. Those days turned out to be some of our best. So many things he had stored up to say, stories he'd been holding onto his whole life, sometimes not even knowing where they came from, or why they should matter to anybody else.

Then one morning he had a stroke and couldn't talk at all. He could still smile a little on one side, glowed sometimes with thanks for being handled with care and gently fed, so Gerty and I knew he was still in there. But now we had to carry on both sides of the conversation, and guess at what he thought and felt. Of course he was frustrated, but with effort slowly regained a little of his power of speech. But the old gabby flow of the months before was gone, and we were under no illusions. We found a nurse, Wendy, who made house calls, came by and spent a few hours a week giving him sponge baths, checking his vitals, making him comfortable. She flirted with him a little, helped us with the medications and let us know what we should be doing next.

But Wes was dwindling, shrinking, now mostly silent and still. One morning Gerty called the ranch to say it was time. She wasn't crying, didn't have much to say, just wanted me out there. I talked to Len Dawes, and took the day off. And barely got there in time to take his hand once more, sit on the edge of the bed and look him square in the eye.

The funeral was mostly a repeat of the surprise party we'd thrown, with a few new folks like Wendy, that we'd met at the doctor's and in hospitals. We buried him on the place, which is still legal in our county, dug the hole ourselves in a grove of trees on the hillside over the garden. I arranged for a big rough chunk of granite that just said Birdsall. There was less singing and dancing, but I repeated that old toast Wes had made, that still seemed to go over. Here's to hay in the mow and the manger, here's to rain on the roof in the winter, here's to keepin' the dirt off your neck while you can.

One day setting on the porch I asked Gerty how she got so lucky, and she looked at me funny. Said There weren't no luck to it, 'cepting maybe the choice to start out with. That first time I let Wes take my hand, lead me out and spread the blanket for that box lunch picnic, he was in no hurry, but so definite, I knew he was the one. From then on, gets so it's just something you do every day, and remember to bring like your hat in the hot sun, and hang on if he'll let you, and hold still if he won't. I said Men often don't know their own minds, and she nodded and said, You can help nudge 'em a little, though you can't make a regular thing of it. We even started cooking together on weekends, one of us baking biscuits or cinnamon rolls, the other scrambling the eggs. We made a few dishes extra-fancy, and laughed over our empty plates like those early days.

Gerty hung on a good while, though she never quite managed much of a life without Wes. She joined the local PTA, and organized bake sales to buy books for the library. I would come around every weekend, spend Saturday and Sunday nights with her. Bought her a TV and a machine that played movies.

In the end I thought too much of the Birdsalls to stay there permanent, and besides, I could see the old boys on the K-Bar needed someone to swap lies and play cards with. When Gerty passed on, we buried her alongside Wes, and threw another party. I still run cattle and horses there, but put up a swing in the yard by Gerty's daffodils, and rented the place to a young couple already raising them a couple kids, that I'm teaching to ride a little on the wild side.

Riding Half a Dream Horse

It was a hard spring rain rare for these parts, that started with a thunderclap just as we were settin' down to flapjacks and eggs in the cook house. Like to woke us up. But then it went on all morning. First rained red mud blown down from the Panhandle out of the north, rusty streaks and splotches slanting across the windows and porch. That for a while turned to sleet and hail that whitened everything. Even the horses out along the corral turned to ghosts that studied us like we might work miracles.

By the time we were done eating, it had settled down to a hard cold rain, that the boys allowed was like a cow pissing on a flat rock. Len Dawes the ramrod said he wanted a word with me, so we made a dash for the barn where behind the tack room he'd made up a little office. We shook off the damp, then Len built a fire in his potbelly stove and made us more coffee. We could hear the gutters and downspouts gurgling and chuckling, and it looked like we might as well hunker down for the wait.

When he got himself comfortable, Len looked up and said Ben, what do you reckon was your first actual horse? He'd already heard a little about Cindy, and my luck with her, off the Lazy B where I did that cooking, but right away I thought of something else.

So I said When I was a boy, for a little while there I wanted a pony. What for, I couldn't say. No one guessed my secret, so none was ever offered. Today I'd say maybe it was a craving for something big and strong to care about, that if I was to treat it right, might carry me off like the wind. But that's just a grownup guess. If I had kids these days I'd have a better notion. But we both know childhood is a distant country, a patchwork of old coats and skirts and whatnot stitched up into a quilt, with every bit of it snatched out of another life, that means you'd have to ask Grandma, then maybe sit around listening all day, so better just forget. Any more I couldn't tell you who I even was back then, much less what a boy might want with a pony, unless it was to start a whole 'nother life. No one I knew had one where we lived in that little clapboard and shingle box on the outskirts of Fresno, that like all our neighbors was an oven in summer and a fridge in winter, with a little fenced-in yard, maybe half an acre of weeds lush in spring, that by mid-summer baked to a dusty hardpan that wouldn't grow nothing and hurt to fall down on.

But I did know where I got this pony notion. It all come in a rush one summer Saturday when I was eight. We didn't have much to do on summer Saturdays, which was Dad's busiest day at the auto body shop. Without him home we mostly watched TV and roamed the neighborhood. Just then a leathery guy in cowboy boots and a big hat and jeans and a vest with some fancy rickarack backed a pony out of a trailer onto our street. It was pulled by an old black Ford pickup with a radiator squared up in front, that he parked there at the curb. When he pulled up and got out I noticed him stealin' a peek or two our way, pretending to be scouting something else. The old cowboy tied the pony to the trailer, and threw him down a little hay. Then he took an empty bucket and sauntered up the walk to our front door. My little brother Donny and baby sister Ginny and I were watching out the front window, and raced to answer his knock. Mother was in the kitchen in back, so we beat her to the punch.

The old cowboy said Howdy and just stood there with the bucket dangling from one fist, that might as well been a space helmet. We didn't mind. We knew what he wanted but had been schooled not to talk to strangers. We stood in a row behind the screen door, struck dumb, studying his grey eyes and mustache. Then a couple heartbeats later here come Mom to see what the dumb show was about. The man snatched his hat off, swooped around and made a little bow as he said Howdy Ma'am, a lovely day we're having. Might I trouble you for the loan of a pail of water for my horse?

We'd never heard a body talk like that. Every single thing he said had a little extra something to it, a spin that made it turn in the sunshine like a windmill brushed with fresh green paint. That out there was no horse, and he wasn't after the loan of a thing, besides which everything he said and did was no trouble in the slightest.

Mom knew what to do. She pushed open the screen door, stuck out her hand and took his, offered him coffee, and told me to go fill the man's pail from the hose at the side of the house. I took the bucket and Donny and Ginny followed me out the front door. At the spigot I ran the water on the lilac bush and forsythia a minute to cool it off and get rid of the rubber

taste, then filled the bucket and sloshed it out to the pony standing in the
street behind the trailer. Right away he lowered his head and drank his fill
while all three of us ventured to pet him, which he didn't seem to mind.
We wondered if he might be a palomino, since his mane and tail were pale
as straw, and he was kind of a tan color. He was a chunky little thing, but
plenty big for us. He had been curried and cared for, and was young and
strong and alive, his mane and tail shining in the sun.

But what do kids know anyhow? We weren't finished petting it when
the cowboy showed up with his coffee still warm in his hand. Mom was
right behind him with her coffee too, smiling and holding one hand up
to shade her eyes. Then she made an announcement: Children, Mr. Buck
Handy here is going to give you all a pony ride.

Mr. Buck Handy polished off his coffee, gave a big smile and nod as
he handed Mom the cup, then went to get a red leather saddle and bridle
out of the bed of the pickup. We watched him spread out and smooth a
little striped blanket on the pony. Right away Ginny asked him What's the
pony's name and he said Lightning. Which suited us just fine. I paid particular attention to how he set the saddle on, reached under the pony's belly
to catch the cinch and pull it across, slid it through a big brass ring and
pulled down, looped it around and slid it under itself to hold tight. Then he
bumped Lightning in the side with his knee, watched till the pony let out a
breath, then pulled that strap as tight as it would get. Then he buckled the
other girth strap, and felt around for the bridle he had hung over his shoulder. He unbuckled the throat latch, fed the pony the bit, worked it back
between his teeth and up over his ears, and buckled the throat latch shut.
But for the rope around the pony's neck, it looked like we were all set.

With that Mr. Buck Handy turned to me, said you must be Ben, and
if you don't mind the oldest should go first to show how it's done. So how's
about you get up in the saddle and we'll take a little ride. He flashed his
big wrinkly smile, in no hurry. He grabbed the left stirrup in his hand and
showed me how to put my left foot in, climb up and swing my right leg
over. Then he showed me how to hold both reins together in my right hand,
and how to turn the pony.

Just like a real cow pony, he feels the opposite rein against his neck.
You don't want to muscle him or hurt his mouth, just give him a sugges-

tion, but make it definite. And when you want to stop, you say whoa and
pull straight back.

With that Mr. Buck Handy turned to tip up a big sign in the bed of the
pickup that said Pony Rides $2, and we were off. Within a minute or two
every kid in the neighborhood was out in their yard watching me ride by.
Within a block every kid was running along the sidewalk, following Lightning and me, with Mr. Buck Handy holding onto the rope so Lightning
couldn't run off.

I felt a little sheepish about that old cowboy hanging on, and also a
little silly in my high-top sneakers and yellow tee shirt. I knew I was no
cowboy, just a kid on a pony, but watching Lightning nod his head and
clop along in the sunshine it was easy to dream. Here I was way up in the
air, and under me the pony felt alive and so did I. When we got to the stop
sign at the second corner Mr. Buck Handy said Why don't you stop him
here. So I said Whoa and pulled back and he stopped. Then Lightning
lifted his tail and lightened his load, and the kids on the sidewalk laughed
at the steaming black pile. Mr. Buck Handy didn't mind, he pointed and
shouted Free Manure! And we all laughed again.

Then Mr. Buck Handy had me turn Lightning around and head back
the way we came. The neighborhood kids were all following, some of the
braver ones dancing pretty close on either side. The old cowboy warned
them off, said Watch out there. You don't want to get stepped on or kicked.
It wouldn't be the poor animal's fault if you got him all upset. But a few of
the bigger boys still kept swooping in till he had to threaten them with the
tail end of the rope coiled in his fist.

When we got back to the pickup and trailer I said whoa and pulled
back, and Lightning stopped. Mr. Buck Handy said Now just get down the
same way you got up. I stood in the stirrups, swung my right leg back over
his tail and got down smooth as pie. He said good job, son, you got the
makings of a real cowboy. Which made me feel great, though my legs felt
so wobbly I sat down on the curb for a minute.

Then Mr. Buck Handy shortened the stirrups and gave my little
brother Donny a hand up in the saddle. He mostly said all the same things
but Donny had been listening, was smart for six, and caught on quick. I
noticed Mr. Buck Handy walked a little closer to the pony's head, which

let Donny know nothing would get out of hand. After a block Donny got a little silly, swinging his legs and saying giddyup, acting like he wanted to go faster. But the old cowboy just ignored that and kept Lightning plodding along in the sunshine, until Donny settled down.

When Donny's ride was done, it was Ginny's turn. She was only four and a half, so Mr. Buck Handy showed her where to put her feet, but then lifted her all the way up into the saddle, with Mom standing on the other side holding out her hands, smiling encouragement. Ginny sat there uncertain for a moment, then started to cry. She reached out for her mother, and Mom took her back down.

There, there now. How about if we just take your picture, dear. Would that be okay, Mr. Handy? It'll only take a minute. Ben, would you run and get the camera out of the kitchen drawer?

So I ran inside for the camera, while they calmed Ginny, then sat her back up in the saddle. She had on a dress anyhow, and looked way out of place aboard Lightning, ignoring the reins, hanging onto the horn for dear life. But we snapped the picture with her smiling bravely, then lifted her down and as soon as the cowboy fiddled with the stirrups, the next kid in line clambered up.

This kid Bobby Jackson lived two blocks over and was in the next grade up from me. He was bigger in every way, kind of a bully who'd shoved his way to the front of the line. He had cowboy boots on, and a red felt cowboy hat with white lacing around the brim. He handed Mr. Buck Handy his money and scrambled up in the saddle, and while the cowboy was busy stuffing his money in a shirt pocket, Bobby kicked Lightning in the ribs with his heels and set off at a gallop that snatched the rope out of the cowboy's hand.

At first it seemed like Bobby knew how to ride, since he got so far ahead of us kids and Mr. Buck Handy chasing him. He was laughing and waving, looking back and taunting us, when all of a sudden he came to that stop sign, at the big cross street where cars didn't have to stop. He turned left and swerved Lightning up onto the sidewalk, which was stupid because there were people out in their yards all along the block. I cut through a yard then up the alley to the center of the block to try to gain on Bobby, and came out just as he was going by. I caught up the rope the pony was dragging and snubbed it around a tree in a yard with no fence, that snapped me against the trunk but stopped them both with a jolt. Lightning reared up, bucking and kicking, and Bobby fell off and lay still. All I could do was hang on until Mr. Buck Handy shuffled up huffing and puffing. I handed him the rope and he said Nice work, and got the pony settled down. Grownups were gathered around Bobby, and got him to sit up. Nothing appeared to be broken, but he wasn't talking much. The kids there all knew whose fault it was, so there wasn't much market for sympathy. I found myself thinking how they used to hang horse thieves but didn't say a thing. The cowboy led the pony back to our place where his gear was, led the pony up into the trailer, and pulled off his saddle and bridle. That looked to be about it for pony rides.

Mom came out of the house with a glass of what looked like lemonade for Mr. Buck Handy. He sure looked like he could use a little something. He probably hadn't run that fast in years. Then as they were standing there in the shade of the trailer Dad drove up in his car, for once home early.

Dad seemed pretty cheery, not tired like he usually was, and mighty interested in whatall was going on. Mom introduced him to Mr. Buck Handy, and the cowboy showed him the pickup and trailer and Lightning and the gear and all, while Mom fetched him a lemonade too. By the time she came out with it, the cowboy was about packed up and set to go. So he started the Ford and waved to us standing there in the yard, pulled a U-turn and drove off.

Mom took Ginny on into the house to fix supper. Donny and I were still hanging around Dad, jabbering away about what a fine animal that pony was, and how he ate and drank and pooped in the street, but how he did what he was told, and how we learned to ride. We just ran on and on a mile a minute. And Dad, that old farm boy, just sat there on the porch and took it in, with a smile fixed on his face. Finally when we stopped a minute to catch our breath, he looked at us and said I hate to tell you boys, but that pony of yours is a mare—which only goes to show some folks don't know the first thing, and some don't care, and we're gonna need to have us a talk about the birds and bees.

Which was about when Len glanced out the window and said Looks like it's fixing to clear up, more's the pity. What do you say we climb up and get that windmill greased while the trough is still full from this rain? So in case we hit a problem it won't mean a doggone thing, since nothing will go thirsty while we're getting it done.

Out Along the Ragged Edge

Len Dawes our foreman was a better farmer than any cowhand cares
to admit. Which is to say he was the best around. He always laid out and
planted the K-Bar's huge garden patch, took charge of the fields we planted
in corn, oats and hay for winter feed. Around him the boys didn't make
the usual cracks about dirt farmers. I took to lending him a hand with the
farming since I never minded the work, that got to be something we had in
common. He didn't talk much about himself, but every time we did farm
work together he let slip a little more. I hadn't been a farm kid myself, but
my father Randy Wilder was, said he'd liked it and missed it. Said it was
real living, if you did it right every bit of it tied to something good for both
you and the neighbors, good for anybody hungry to be fed.

One fall stretch of nice weather we were baling and bucking the last
of the hay, hauling in a final heavy load that we'd piled too high to save
another trip with the wagon and team, so tossed a couple lines over it and
had to take it slow. Took over an hour teetering along from the field to the
barn. Driving the team along in dreamy slow motion, Len asked if I'd ever
worked mules. I told him I couldn't say as I knew much about 'em, but
for that one season on the Lazy B, driving chuck wagon, cooking for fall
roundup. I had liked that mule team, Mutt and Jeff, that gave me an easy
time of it. All they took was a little attention and patience.

Len said That's how I see 'em too. Always liked mules myself, though
they don't all have such an easy motion to saddle and ride. Some are stiff-
legged. But there are some good ones, sure-footed and sensible as the day is
long. Then, reins in hand, as we eased along dodging rocks and holes, for
the first time he spoke of his childhood.

Said I grew up outside Collinwood, Tennessee, toward Lutts, near
where the Natchez Trace run north, heading up into Nashville. I got a good
start back there, I see now. For a while there we didn't know we was poor,
before we kids started school. Goat-footed, owl-eyed, in mended hand-me-
downs, no matter, those were the best years of our lives—mine, anyhow—
before I knew what was what. My dad rented this run-down old farm for

the house on it, then saw it had just about everything a body might need
to feed us—forty acres with a barn and sheds, and all manner of rusty
implements. The landlord said The land was played out long ago, but you're
welcome to poke around, make what you can of it. The first couple years
Dad worked off the rent, shingled the house and barn, patched and painted,
dug ditches, mended fence. Dad found an old black sharecropper neighbor Ernie Poole, that folks called Ernie Peaches for his kindly disposition,
who'd sell him the one thing he had most need of, a mule. The deal was one
payment a year, at harvest, for as long as it took. Took five years to pay off
that mule, but Ernie Peaches never minded, and the mule never wore out,
kept on smart and strong.

As a little kid I sure admired that mule, that could do anything my dad
might think to ask. His name was Mac, and he didn't talk no more than
what I did. At four and five I plain wanted to be Mac, wanted his name
for my own, liked the sound of it, wanted to plod and pull like him, and
kick up my heels like him when the day's work was done. Mac would spend
Sundays turned out with Trudy, Ernie Peaches' other mule. They'd stand
in the shade head to tail and switch flies, which practically looked like true
love.

Our place had an old McClellan cavalry saddle with no horn, with
USA and the date 1882 stamped in the leather skirt. It was the first I ever
rode, before I got my first real pair of shoes, and the stirrups hurt my feet.
Mac stood still for me to saddle him, never had to be trained or broke,
let me clamber up and just go. We had no idea how old he was. That was
home, the only one I knew, the one I'd take even now if it was offered.
Every spring I'd follow the old man and Mac plowing up and down, watch
what turned up in the rows and stuff it in my pockets—flint arrowheads
and ax heads and heavy rocks all burnt to a cinder, that we called shooting
stars.

Then one day everything changed. Dad had got the plow stuck in
some tree roots along one edge of the field, that stopped Mac cold. The old
man was late getting crops in, on account of a wet rainy stretch that kept
coming, never really dry enough to plow. A couple times a day he'd have to
unhitch the plow, and pull Mac out of a wallow dug in up to his belly. This
time he took a step or two toward the mule, shrugged off the plow lines

96

looped over one shoulder and under the other. Then he took the big knot at the ends of those lines to that mule, shouting and switching him like it was all Mac's fault. I could never stand to see an animal beaten, still can't, and this was the first. I ran to try and stop him, but Dad backhanded me ass over teakettle, and kept after Mac. I turned around and went back to the house, never told a soul, but never followed him out to the field again. After dark I went out to check Mac over, and take him a treat, a couple fermented fall apples out of the bottom of the barrel. He seemed fine, just a little skittery. I watched them from a distance from then on. It took forever for Mac to get over it. Maybe he never did.

Then pretty quick I started school, first grade, got new britches that fit, and my first real pair of shoes. In short order I came to see my family as others saw us, as poor hardworking nobodies, called white trash by some behind our backs, mostly living out along the ragged edge. I was the second child, always seen as the good one who minded, never had to be told twice, where the eldest, my brother Willy, two years older, was kind of a hell-raiser who joshed and joked with everyone. Did what he felt like soon as he got big enough and quick enough. Yet at heart Willy was a good boy, I knew he meant no harm, and I would ache for him, like I did for Mac. That way Willy had of making folks laugh was a pure gift. He could make up a joke out of thin air, nothin' but a goat fart, and dare you not to crack up.

I never even knew my dad had a hard side, till he walloped that mule. He'd been kind and playful and gentle with us when we were small. But from then on I was watchin' for it, and seemed to see it everywhere. Hard words and a hard hand from someone who seemed stuck, angry at what his life was giving him. Like he was sure there oughta be more, but then where would that come from, what would it even look like?

Finally, things between my brother Willy and my dad came to a head. In his junior year Willy wanted to quit school and get him a job. He'd goofed off enough that the classes had got hard. He'd been skating along, squeakin' by. Now here came his fall report card, that the parents had to sign. The old man said he'd need to knuckle down. Willy told them he wanted to quit and find him a job. Dad said No way, nohow, he was going to get good grades, and graduate. No surprise, that night Willy run off. Found a job at a service station pumping gas, doing oil changes, patching tires, that kinda thing, and slept on a cot in the back. A neighbor boy told me where he was, and I went to visit him one day after school, though it meant walking five miles to the next town over, and catching hell when I got home after dark. Willy had on a little green cloth cap and coveralls, and was changing a fan belt on a big blue Oldsmobile. He was the only one there. Whenever someone drove over the rubber line out front and rang the bell, he had to run to pump gas.

When we finally got a minute, I told him I missed him, and asked him what he was doin'. He said Savin' up to get shut of here. So then I said Where you goin', what you gonna do? He said I'm headin' for Californy, that the hobos sing about. Where they sleep out every night, and it's like the promised land, things grow so big and sweet. Pretty soon I was beggin' him to take me along, but he wouldn't, said I had a future here and mustn't ruin it.

On the long walk home to supper I thought it out, and remembered something else. Most of the kids around Collinwood had to move away to get a job anyhow. So high school graduation had got to be one big bittersweet goodbye, that felt like the finish of everything. Few ever made it to college, and few new jobs ever came out our way, except for the first big-box stores that would just about finish what was left of small towns a few years further on.

If seeing Dad hit that mule changed some things, that talk with Willy did the rest. Set me on the path to askin' what I should want for myself. From then on I was biding my time and keepin' my trap shut. One of my teachers at school said I showed promise, should apply for a college scholarship. Meanwhile my folks seemed like they'd both given up, and were settling into a grim kinda quiet, that every now and again would explode. Which upset the little ones. Those two little girls, Ruthie and Minnie, were the sweetest kids. But I couldn't fix it for them, any more than I could for Willy. I knew I had all I could handle just looking after myself.

So I stuck it out at school, and sometimes rode that mule of an evening to parties, even though some kids would laugh. But strange to say Dad and Mom didn't mind me takin' the mule, and Mac put up with me, waited and watched for each night to be done, tied to a fence, or off in the bushes somewhere. I'd bring him a treat from the party, a cupcake or something, then on the long ride home tell him how it had been and what was what.

Meanwhile Willy got so he knew all about cars. He'd come by home when he was out testing one he'd just fixed, toot the horn and stop a minute to let the folks know he's alive. He'd tell the little girls this shiny new car was his, but I knew it wasn't so, and would tell them later he had just been kidding, but was getting to be a real mechanic. When he met a girl named Jenny Morrissey who liked to go out dancing, he quit talking about heading off to California, and told me he wasn't saving so much anymore. But he'd planted the seed, and I decided after graduation I'd be heading west myself.

By the time graduation rolled around, I'd been putting a little money aside from odd jobs. Dad and Mom and the girls came all dressed up, in the old pickup truck Dad had bought. They were proud of me, I could see that, and I got to make a little speech to the class and parents and teachers, that was a little too serious for my own good, entitled The Hope of the Future, which I took to be us. I told them it was a shame we all had to leave, but the world had no room for us here. By the time I was done it was deathly quiet, then burst into wild applause, mostly the graduates themselves. When the principal handed me my diploma, he muttered that he'd like to talk some time, but I just nodded and moved on.

I went to the final party that night, out of town by the old Hobb's Hill limestone quarry. There was a lot of noisy drinking around a bonfire, too far out for neighbors or cops to bother with. Turned out I was some kind of hero, was going to get quoted in tomorrow's newspaper. A few solid citizens had talked it up, said something ought to be done, but there wasn't much to offer by way of real jobs with any kind of a future.

The one real surprise at the quarry was my brother Willy, who'd crashed the party to see what I was going to do next. I pulled him aside and said I was still heading west. He said How about I give you a ride as far as Memphis? Since there'd never been much traffic going past Collinwood in any direction, I said that would be great. The next morning he came by to get me, and I had my stuff in a little cardboard suitcase with a busted latch all tied with rope. I had a little less than two hundred bucks in my pockets and shoes, and was set to go. Dad pulled me aside and said You know you don't have to go, there'll always be a place here for you. I knew his offer wasn't real, there was only room for a helper who'd work for free and bite his tongue, about like Mac, really, so I shook his hand and thanked him, and hugged my mom, and scooped up Ruthie and Minnie and told them both to behave, like that would fix a thing. Then I got into the shiny new Chevy Willy was driving and we pulled away. In the rush to be gone I even forgot to tell old Mac goodbye.

On the drive Willy and I had the most serious talk we'd ever had. He liked being a mechanic but was starting to see the drawbacks of a dirty job that required a big expensive set of tools. His girlfriend ran hot and cold about his prospects, although he was doing his best. As for myself, I admitted I didn't have a clue, but was going to find something to do and see where it got me. As we were pulling into Memphis I said how about leaving me off at the stock yards, on the south side of town up against the railroad tracks. When we got there I climbed out and thanked him, and he sat and watched me till I was out of sight.

When I got to the stockyard's big front gate I turned in, climbed up on the overhead walkway and went along looking over the livestock. I'd heard about it but had never been here, in fact I'd never been to Memphis, though it was less than two hours away.

Then all at once I saw something I knew all about, together with something I'd never seen before. I saw a cowboy looking up at me. He was riding a big black mule.

I waved and yelled down, Nice mule. He laughed and twirled his lariat. In this maze of chutes and pens he was running calves along while someone up ahead opened a gate and turned them in. This appeared to be something I could do, so I looked around for the nearest stairs down to the stock pens. When I got down where the cowboy was, I said What's your mule's name? He said I'm not sure. Troubador, or Lancelot, or Jezebel. I forget. What's your name, mule? Troubador? The mule shook its head. Lancelot? The mule shook its head again. Then I guess you must be Jezebel. The mule shook its head a third time. We both laughed, then he said, Oh, now I recollect. Your name is Miniver. At that the mule nodded its big head up and down.

I introduced myself, and the cowboy reached down to shake my hand, said he was Stacy Hicks. Then he said And you already met my mule. I looked at the cowboy and we both laughed again. It's like here was a billboard with my name on it. I knew right then I could do anything Stacy could, or could figure it out in no time. And wanted to be a cowboy. I had no idea how long the road might be, how much time and work it might take, but that was it.

I spent two nights with Stacy Hicks. Slept on his couch, ate doughnuts and coffee with him, admired all he had, which was a saddle and a lariat, a big hat and boots that were black to match his mule. That all agreed with me. After two days Stacy found me a ride west with a trucker named Chuck O'Meera in a big diesel cattle hauler full of feeder calves. Chuck was heading for Kansas City, then got another load on to Fort Worth, and I just tagged along. Pure dumb luck was all it was, living on hamburgers, coffee and pie.

Twice I crawled into the truck to run the calves out for him, smelled pretty ripe from the calf shit but it washed right off. By the time Chuck headed out of the Forth Worth yards to pick up a load on a spread in West Texas, I was sleeping in the truck, and calling the turns on the map for him. After helping load the cows, I asked the foreman on the Table Rock Ranch for a job. Which was just more of the same dumb luck. Within two years I was head wrangler on the place, in charge of the remuda, then just grew into the rest by paying attention, letting the livestock show me what was what.

For that last little bit of Len's story we sat in the shade in front of the barn, the team standing quiet, in no hurry to unload.

Feeling Halfway Home

Annalise was waitressing at the place where I stopped for coffee, off and on, halfway out to my little ranch. I didn't know much about her, but liked what I saw. I still called my ranch the Birdsall place a dozen years after the final payment was made, which is to say that although they had both passed on, the fine old couple and the projects we'd done left their mark.

This little spot known as Henry's Crook was nothing much, a gas station the one thing left standing of a settlement named for the first settler on this road, Henrick Benson, at a deep bend in the Rio Concho that never dried up. Folks all said he stopped and stayed here for the murky but drinkable water. It was here the serpentine old river road T-boned into State Route 6, the only road anywhere near the west side of the K-Bar ranch where I worked. Someone had converted the station's two service bays into an eatery with a kitchen, a counter, booths and tables that caught a blend of the morning sun and cool shadows that by midmorning managed to lure fishermen in off the river. The old boys would grumble over eggs and coffee about why they weren't biting this time. There was always something—a gullywasher that had silted the river, or a hot dry spell that shrunk it to a stretch of disconnected pools, or a thunderstorm that somehow got hung up in the Sangre de Cristo range to the west, not like a ghost train flickering its heat-lightning, passing over in the night. The fishermen were mostly retired city folk who'd grown up somewhere else, back east, up north or out in California, and most weren't too bothered by the lack of fish. There were no prodigious lunkers to be landed here anyhow, and some even liked that the river's denizens were elusive, hard to catch. From my experience it was mostly a matter of temperature—these fellas should just stick a thermometer in the river, and if it read over eighty degrees on a clear sunrise forget it.

The big overhead doors on the two bays would be closed in the mornings, unless the weather was unusually fine. This morning it was cool, with the woods showing fall colors, and a little breeze stirring. There was usually someone in early to sell gas, make coffee, sell frozen bait and nightcrawlers out of the chest freezer and fridge by the register. The kitchen got going about 6:30, which is when a pair of county deputies usually set up camp in a booth to eat breakfast, gossip, swill coffee and do their nightshift paperwork. When I saw their cruiser parked in the shade to one side, I usually stopped, if only to hear the latest and keep on their good side.

Then there was Annalise, who seemed glad to see me, her eyes sparkling after half a year off. I put my hat on the wide shelf over the coathooks near the door, and waited till she put me somewhere she wanted me to be.

It hadn't always been that way. We'd first met when I stopped there several times as spring was just coming on, but I still recalled practically the last thing she'd said directly to me. Not everybody knows about horses or wants to, she'd said, and gave me a withering look as I'd backed the second mare out of the trailer. She had walked up to me in the gravel parking lot which was mostly empty, and said What are you doing? I wasn't a smart-mouth, didn't say What does it look like. Wasn't prickly or abrupt, just matter-of-fact. I'd said They've been in the box all morning in the sun while I been stuck in a line at the courthouse. I thought I'd give 'em a stretch and a look around. To which she said I wish you'd asked us first. Then I said what I wished I hadn't. I said If this ain't horse country no more, nowhere is—so just tell me. Then right away I stopped and turned back around to stammer my apologies, which she met with a shrug and sailed off. So I tied my horses to cleats along the trailer, went in and got coffee and a muffin to go, came out, fed my horses each a handful of muffin, loaded up and tore out. And didn't even slow down coming past Henry's Crook for another half a year.

But then today as I swung by I noticed something new—a galvanized water tank under a shade tree by the parking lot, alongside a hitching rail, near where the boat ramp leads down to the river. There was even a horse saddled and tied there. So I slowed to pull over and ease the pickup back around into the lot. Maybe it was a sign.

Or maybe I was in the mood for redemption. I hadn't been set down this hard, or been this wrong about my attraction to someone in forever. Annalise hadn't ever said all that much, but every time I'd looked her way she was looking right back at me. Maybe she was just afraid of horses, took a bad spill when she was young, that she was just now getting over. You had to learn to work and play around these big, strong, shy critters. Folks got bit and kicked and stepped on, and some thought it must be the horse to blame. But maybe someone was moving too quick or acting too goofy for their own good. Or the horse couldn't see what was coming his way, and had read the sign wrong. So I came in to find out which it might be, and see if we couldn't turn that bad feeling around.

When Annalise came to bring me a menu, I said That's a nice-lookin' mare out there—is she yours? She just shook her head, but never took her eyes off me. So I got to ask how long the trough and hitching rail had been out there, and she said A week maybe. I said Well I appreciate it, and if you don't mind I'll spread the word. The boys all like havin' someplace to ride, where they can tie up their horse in the shade halfway home and get some water. Then I asked her how she'd been, and she said Fine, but was still pretty quiet, which wasn't all a bad sign.

Here we were into October, with the summer come and gone. It seemed a little early for the cast-iron stove, even with the door propped open. But I stepped in front of it and spread my hands to the heat. My joints and knuckles thanked me.

Watching Annalise behind the counter across the diner I tried to recall what else we'd even talked about. I had just turned 50 when we met, and was feelin' my years, feelin' halfway home still a ways from where I'd hoped to get, wondering if there was one more dance left in me, not just the long ride. I remember trying to explain to her why some like me talked to their ponies, what they said and meant, and what they didn't mean. Like dogs, horses mostly just knew your tone of voice, and a word or two. Gee and haw, giddyup and whoa. Maybe barn, maybe oats, maybe saddle. Some horses liked singing. The tone and tune were everything. For an innocent shy creature, all they wanted was to please you and flee trouble and get fed.

Annalise had thought that mostly foolishness, and said so. I had smiled and shrugged, and why not. Here I was back talking horses with a pretty woman near my age who didn't seem to mind shootin' the breeze. Sometimes you knew what you knew and had to wait out the ones who took their time but got there eventually. She was sure easy to look at in the meantime, easy to set and watch, be around when she smiled back. She had that dark curly hair she said she trimmed herself a couple times a year, that she said still had bounce if she didn't let it get too long. It had a few streaks of silver to it, that caught the blue-gray of her eyes, and her eyes had crows-feet deepened by her tan, that said she spent time outdoors without sunglasses doing something that was nobody's business or she'd a told 'em. I couldn't quite figure what that was, and was not about to go straight at it, with things between us now getting on so nice and easy.

So after breakfast and extra coffee, on a whim I asked if she'd ever ridden a horse, and when she looked at me funny but didn't answer, I ventured ahead and asked if she'd like to take a ride on her day off, which I knew to be Mondays. Said we could make it an outing, a picnic. Might be fun. And she said yes.

So two days later I pulled up to Henry's Crook first thing, with that same horse trailer, and when she stepped up, her first question was Where'd you get the horses? I said These are a couple I raised up offa my little place. Which is a good hour from where I work.

"And where is that?" She looked at me with that hard steady eye that felt like it could bore right through me.

"The K-Bar place. What? I say something wrong?"

"Just yesterday I asked Deputy Larrabee where a body would go to find cowboys around here, and he went on about all the deadbeats and drunks and show ponies he mostly sees on his rounds. Rambled on till I said I had an order up. When I turned away he finally said I don't know what you're lookin' for, but the real ones are out at the K-Bar."

"You don't say."

"Well, that's not me, that's Roy Larrabee."

"Good to hear anyhow."

I had a lunch packed in my saddlebags, but pulled out a thermos for coffee that I paid Annalise to go behind the counter and fill, since Henry's was known to brew better coffee than what we made at the ranch, that still favored eggshells and a pinch a salt. Then we headed off. It was cool fall weather, but still sunny and dry, and I aimed to make the most of it.

In the truck I was able to check out how she dressed, in worn jeans and boots and what looked like a fancy snap-button shirt all stitched with vines and leaves. Over that she had a heavy sweater, and a serious wide-brim felt hat. The only thing I had to ask was if she had gloves, and she did, in a hip pocket.

For the ride I'd brought Peaches and Hank, the pair of foals we'd raised out at the Birdsall place. Now nine year-olds, they were the easiest and gentlest riding pair I had. They liked each other and liked me, and had both been ridden by Gerty Birdsall back when they were just getting started, so knew where to put their feet, and how to do whatever might be asked.

I wasn't going to take her riding on my little place, that wasn't big enough to let her feel like we were going much of anywhere, and the K-Bar was plenty big but crawling with hands who worked with me and would be prone to stare and gossip, so I thought of a place that had some real vistas, though not much by way of rough climbs or trails. It was a stretch of state open range land where the plains slowly tilted till you could see off to the south about a hundred miles. And since it was fall there might be no one much to bother us.

It took an hour to get to the start of this range land, then another little while till we found a wide spot in the road to park and unload. I wanted the horses to like Annalise from the get-go, so I handed her a paper sack with some apples to seal the deal. I made a little dumb show of how to offer an apple with my palm flat, fingers together. I looked a question at her, and she nodded and smiled back.

Then I got the horses out, tied them alongside the trailer, and told Annalise to get acquainted while I tossed out the gear and got them saddled up. She laughed at me gently, then sidled up next to Peaches, patted and fussed over her a bit. She didn't seem nervous in the least, in fact she seemed like she knew what she was doing, and liked the attention the horse was giving her.

When she'd given each of the horses an apple, we mounted up for the ride, with me on Hank, and Peaches happily nodding and swishing her tail to be carrying this friendly newcomer. As I expected, for most of the ride there were no trails. The range here was quietly overwhelming, the southern horizon the earth's own faint curve, with few landmarks anywhere near, with nothing but killdeers calling off in the distance, and a red-tailed hawk circling and letting out a scream before she tucked her wings and dropped. We stopped to watch her tear into the jackrabbit she'd hit, then clicked our tongues and moved on. We didn't talk, there just didn't seem much need, with the horses content to ease along and pace themselves step for step.

At one point Annalise stirred Peaches into a canter, and Hank and I kept with her, just a few paces behind. I didn't feel the need to lead, and didn't intrude on one of a cowhand's elementary pleasures, running easy into an open future with no obstructions or boundaries anywhere in sight. It was rare these days but shouldn't be. Who'd bother saying this is how it mostly used to be, when here it still is today?

Even the horses seemed awed, humbled and charged by the long day in this vast expanse, with its fall mostly yellows, browns and reds, but still a smattering of green. Half-brother and half-sister from the same sire, born a day apart, the horses were used to setting out and stopping on the same foot, used to living in tandem, being startled and moved and drawn to identical things.

After a couple hours we could begin to see a sprinkling of cattle in the distance, and I started looking for a place to step down and have lunch. I pointed toward a thin line of small trees that marked some kind of water course, and we came onto a low patch where the ground cover wasn't so sparse. We reined up and tumbled down to stretch our legs, and let the horses try the grass here. I tossed down their saddles and blankets, undid their bridles and staked them out in halters at either end of my lasso, that I'd looped around a tough little juniper. Then I laid out the spread for lunch on a Hudson's Bay blanket. It was nothing fancy, some burritos and enchiladas I'd made and wrapped in towels to keep warm. I pulled the cork on a bottle of a Spanish wine, a Sangre de Toro, and dug out cups for that and coffee.

Turns out we were both famished, and ate just about everything in sight. Luckily I had brought olives and pickled beans and carrots, and humus and tortillas, that went well with the wine. I cut up the best apple we had left to share, then gave the others to Hank and Peaches.

Annalise was still smiling but finally seemed too quiet and I asked if anything was wrong. She said she was overwhelmed at how perfect the day had turned out. Then she said It's a little like being in church. Like you're waiting for your heart to speak, to dare break the silence of God.

I told her I wasn't sure I knew what that meant, but felt it clear as a birdsong. I thought maybe we could both do without much more jabber, but didn't say so.

Then she said I've got something to show you. She unsnapped her shirt pocket and pulled out an old black and white photograph and handed it to me. It was a shot of a girl on a pony, and a man beside her on a tall horse. The girl was facing the camera, but the man was looking away. They were both sitting English saddles, and the girl wore jodhpurs and high black boots, with a little jacket that must have been red, and a fuzzy black hard hat. The girl's stare was hard to miss. It was Annalise at eleven or twelve.

I pointed and said This is you and your father? She nodded.

I thought you said you hadn't ridden before, though it appears you have. What's the story?

I just didn't answer when you asked.

Then I guess I just didn't hear what you didn't say.

She was looking at me hard again. I couldn't tell if she might laugh or cry. She said I was stunned at how long it had been. But Peaches let me know it's always just today. And back there in the parking lot I wasn't angry at you, I was mad at my father. It just boiled up outa me. It didn't come out like it was supposed to, and was over before I could stop it. I came out to apologize but don't know how you got out of there so fast.

Felt like I'd got scalded. Is your dad still alive?

No. But over the years we worked some things out.

What was wrong? Can you put a finger on it?

Annalise shrugged. Then she laid it out, how she was what she called an Army brat, who had been raised all over, ten schools in twelve years, by a father who at the time she left home was a colonel in the armored cavalry. Her mother always went her own way, and kept her own counsel. Her dad had been brought along by a bunch of old-school cavalry officers who all still rode horses on the least excuse. She said It's like sailing with the Navy, the officers learn to sail at Annapolis to really know the basics. Horses are just what they had before tanks, to make quick tactical moves in rough country, and beat infantry to the punch.

I was still looking at the picture of that serious, intense girl on her pony, who seemed poker-faced, even a bit defiant.

Did you like it?

I liked the horses, though they could be a mixed blessing. I was always afraid of getting hurt. And one other thing—I didn't like how hard Dad was on his horses. He always rode the biggest strongest ones he could find, and was rough with them. So his horses were always edgy and afraid.

Were you scared of him too?

All the while I was growing up. He was no fun to be around. Had a temper that got the better of him, seemed like he loved to shout orders, recite chapter and verse and deal out punishment--then he'd be sorry next morning. So impatient and critical. He blamed his moods on what he called command indoctrination. Had no time for much else.

Finally she got around to it, as we both knew she would. Why had she been so mad at me? It turns out because I reminded her of him. She even said I looked like him, though I couldn't see it in the photo. It's for sure I didn't act like him, though I must have let my impatience show when she challenged me unloading those two mares.

At that point I took a break to get up and move the horses off to the west a hundred yards, and wound their rope around another little scrub tree. Their tails showed how happy they were. They'd run out of things to pick over and taste right here, and appreciated the change.

Then I sat back down on the blanket, that suddenly felt more like I climbed aboard something, since there it lay with us like a raft on an ocean. All this emptiness, waving grasses on the prairie stirred by a little wind. The sun was sinking toward the west, and I hadn't brought a light. Which is what I was thinking when she leaned over and kissed me.

I grinned and said Huh, and kissed her right back.

What were you worried about?

I told her I just didn't want this day to end, and had forgot to bring a light.

She looked up and around, and gave a little laugh. Then said There's a piece of moon that's gonna be rising while the sky is still light. Besides, the horses will find the way.

Yeah?

Have they been here before?

No.

It's no matter. This is their place, their heaven. Here they know better than we do.

We rolled around on the blanket till sundown, tasting the moment and each other, a little giddy at how far we'd come. Then over us came roll on roll of blazing clouds, of reds and purples and golds, that seemed to hover but changed every time we looked down at each other. When it was done we packed and stepped up in the saddle in the afterglow, all lavender and rose. It was a long quiet ride in the dark, with half a moon rising just like she'd said. We gave the horses their heads, and they were glad to be next to each other, nodding in perfect agreement. The cool air still held a little of the night song of cicadas and nightjars and whatnot. In the dark she'd steer Peaches close, reach out her gloved fingertips and touch my shoulder and knee. We made it back just fine, and I let her out of the truck at Henry's Crook right about ten.

We only went on a couple more rides after that— as fall wound down tried and failed to rekindle the magic. We'd made a start, but what I didn't know about her would fill haylofts. I never knew where she called home, never heard her young ambitions and dreams. Didn't know if Henry's Crook was her high point or low point, the start or end of something—or just a wide spot off a back road where something caught up with her a min-ute. I knew only two things for sure--she'd had horses in her life. And when she saw me, every time she looked right at me hard and long, and never looked away.

Turned out that was not enough. We were not so compatible as we thought. She was fine with Peaches and Hank, that I'd been counting on, but she still had a thing about men. That apparently weren't to be trusted, no matter what they said and did.

Night Watch

The three of us were out riding fence. The two new boys Deano and
Willy were with me to get the lay of the land, learn how we did things. See
did they want to swap the coal shovel folds on their hat brims for the round
old way I wore mine. It was after spring roundup, and we'd already had a
few storms, but there were forty-some odd miles of fence on this season's list
left to check, maybe fix. This wouldn't be the grinding breakneck pace of
driving and cutting cattle, though it paid not to be careless. So we brought
along a big mule to pack tools and a couple new rolls of wire, and each of
us led a spare horse just in case. After a long day's ride, late in the day we'd
come up on the far fence, had turned to follow its four strands of smooth
eleven-gauge wire, and would be working our way back home heading
north then east.

Among our regular hands we'd had one hand break his elbow on the
spring drive, and another off tending his mother who had gone under the
knife for stomach cancer, so Len Dawes had hired these two boys, and
asked me to take them under my wing and get them started right. And they
were purely curious. Willy wanted to know what the boys did for fun. I
mentioned horseshoes and cards, and the spectacle of pretty girls weekend
nights at the Rustlers' Corral, and the rodeo events some favored, on into
summer and fall. Deano wanted to know where to get a pair of the chaps I
was wearing. Said they looked like buffalo. I told him they were Highland
cowhide, a hardy red long-haired breed from Scotland, and the gettin' place
was Syd's Outerwear in El Paso, but bring a satchel of money. I was trying
to be straight with him, but when you're green the truth can sound like a
bad joke. Some things you need to learn for yourself, and the sooner the
better.

When we hired on a new hand, one thing they did for sure the first
year was ride the outer fence line around the whole place. A little over a
hundred and twelve miles. That's the only way to see where the water comes
and goes, how the cattle and horses live out of sight of us, and where weak

spots in the fencing might be. On the K-Bar there are only two fences—
that outer one that encircles the whole seven hundred eighty odd square
miles, and an inner one that keeps the cattle and horses out of the people's
business, the yards and garden, fields of hay, corn, oats and beans. There
are corrals large and small, and a few pastures fenced and gated, for breeding purposes and for weaning calves. For twenty years we've been replac-
ing barbed wire with eleven-gauge smooth wire, to keep from tearing up
livestock, but it's a work in progress.

It was already late so I set them to water and feed the horses, gave them
a hint to each take two at a time and lead them down to the creek, while
I built a fire and threw some supper together, chili cheese dogs and beans,
and got set for the night, planning on an early start. Over dinner somehow
the question came up, what it meant to be a top hand. How did you get to
be one, and what was the difference in pay? Deano asked was I getting paid
for the cooking, for instance, and I said not really, though being a top hand
meant I could do anything on the place, so got paid for taking the lead.
With a top hand there were generally no excuses. Things got done without
fumbling and grumbling. Given a little time, they would see how it worked.

Once we were settled down into our bags, I lay there enjoying the
night, tuning into it like it was an old radio, sometimes catching static,
sometimes one clear song, leaned back against my saddle, looking up and
out. Some coyotes were yipping back and forth, one den of pups singing
out to another out of pure lonesomeness. Once in a great while far off a
mountain lion would scream, hushing even the peepers and crickets. There
were cattle in the distance too, now and then calves and cows split up in
the dark, bawling for each other. The ponies along the picket line were a
constant sleepy commotion, stamping, shaking and pawing in their sleep, a
drowsy force of creation like the soundless tumble and drift of blurred stars
out along the Milky Way. Every little while a shooting star would streak
across the sky, flare up and die.

The dark was mostly how I liked it, restless and alive, taking no notice
of a few sleepy cowhands sprawled out underfoot. Here we weren't the boss
of anything, which felt about right. At least we weren't lying right in the
trail to be stepped on.

Then like an eye rolling open, the sky was the pearl gray of morning.

114

I set the boys to feed and water the ponies, while I stirred up the fire, got coffee and flapjacks going. Then we packed and mounted up to follow the fence. And in an hour or two had our hands more than full.

First was the track of a storm through a thicket that had snatched up a handful of trees that in turn flattened thirty feet of fence. I put the boys to work pulling steeples, setting and tamping posts back up, cutting a couple new ones from the best of the blown-down trees. While they were busy I went down through the gap to look for tracks, see if any cattle had found this hole and passed either way. The grass was always greener, as ranchers and farmers would say, and the cattle were naturally curious. But I could only find one small set of tracks, that had come uphill through the opening, that I let Jericho follow a ways to see what might turn up. And sure enough, only half a mile away, hid deep in a thicket we found a young heifer in trouble.

She was a likely-looking little girl, a red and white Hereford with a short face and big dark eyes, though right now she looked more than a little panicked. The cause wasn't far to seek. She was big as a barn and about to calve. Her bag was full and her teats were dripping, her cervical plug was hanging down and one tiny rear hoof was sticking out of her vulva, baby mostly turned the right way, but mama hadn't been here before so had no notion, and was breathing hard. There were no other cattle around for miles. She hadn't been tagged or branded, so at the moment belonged to the K-Bar as much as anyone. I put a halter on her, talked to her a little and stroked her to calm her, coaxed her out and tied her to a tree in a clearing, and went back to tell the boys. We got the fence shut tight in short order, then brought the horses and the mule along to where the heifer was.

I asked if either of them had ever pulled a calf and both shook their heads no. So pay attention, I said, this is top hand stuff. I do a couple dozen of these a year. I unpacked the vet bag and got everything laid out on a tarp. Took off my hat, vest, shirt and chaps, hung them on a tree, leaving only my undershirt and jeans, and pulled on a long blue glove that went up to my armpit and over my shoulder, and tied on a plastic butcher's apron over that. Then while I smeared my glove with a tube of lubricant, I told Willy and Deano they should ask questions whenever they thought of one, but not to worry if I couldn't answer right away, since some of this was a matter of timing, getting the right things done when they come due. I took some soft double-braid line and tied one end to the hoof we could see, then reached in to see what was what.

The baby's kicking, I said. And I can feel a pulse. Then I reached around to where the other leg and hoof were hung up on the ledge of the mama's pelvic arch, folded the leg close under the baby, pushed it back in to get room to straighten the leg out through the vulva, then tied the other end of the soft rope around the baby's second hoof. Then I reached in to straighten out the baby's tail, and hooked the calf puller's handles onto the two ropes, and got set to deliver the baby. But one more thing first. I fixed two syringes with epinephrine, to help her uterus relax. Tapped on the muscles around her hip joints to loosen them up, then drove in the plunger and rubbed on each shot.

I started telling the boys what I was doing as I did it. You always want mama up on her feet. You want the baby's spine parallel to mama's, both pointing up. You want to lube up the baby so she slides easy. You want to pull at a slight angle down, so as not to hang up the baby's head on the roof of the pelvis. And make sure the baby's tail is running straight out between its legs. You can deliver a baby breach, coming out nose-first, but it's a little tricky. You don't ever want to pull on the head if you can help it. Best to pull on the hooves once you've got the legs straightened out. If there's no room to turn the baby around, pull on the front legs, with the nose tucked down.

I had her all lubed up and ready, and showed them where to watch her muscles contracting, how mama was pushing, said I was waiting to pull with her, and help her get this done. Three, four, five steady pulls, then all of a sudden the calf slid out at our feet, in a gush of water and blood. I cleared away the afterbirth, picked up the calf and hung its head down over the low limb of a nearby tree, opened the calf's mouth to clear its airway, picked up a straw to tickle one nostril then the other, until the baby coughed and took its first breath.

When it was moving a little, its eyes fluttering, I went back to the mama and put my gloved arm all the way in to feel around. Willy said Now what're you doing, and I answered Looking for any more placenta. Then all

at once I grinned and said Surprise. Willy said What? I said I thought she
still looked too big around for a little backcountry heifer. She's got twins. I
asked Willy to untie the lines from the first baby's hind feet, while I got the
other one straightened out. It took a little work, but mama's contractions
were slowly moving the second calf back to her pelvic opening. I got the
two back hooves turned right with the tail straight out between them, then
straightened up the front legs to streamline the second calf. We got the lines
tied around the baby's back legs at the hocks, then put the handles on and
pulled, and rode and let up with her contractions till twenty minutes later I
eased the second baby out onto the ground.

This one wasn't breathing either. I felt for a pulse, then hung her up
and tried my tricks, but it was no go. I would have to work quick, and
breathe for her. So I got down and covered her mouth and one nostril with
my palm and my thumb, and filled her lungs by blowing into the other nostril. All the while I rubbed her chest under her left front leg, right over her
heart. Come on, little one, breathe.

It was a close thing, but you don't want to give up while there's a
chance. This was a smart little heifer whose offspring might do the world
some good. I just hoped we hadn't got there too late, or waited too long.
I told the boys we were keeping the first calf away from mama so she
wouldn't reject the second one, since it always worked better if they bonded
together, all at once. So I kept blowing its lungs full of air, squeezing its
chest and rubbing its heart till that damp dark little thing coughed and
sneezed itself into life. Then we wiped off both the calves with gunny sacks
and set them in front of mom to see what she made of them. And right
away she sniffed and nudged and licked them off while we moved away
to the far end of the clearing, pretending not to watch, just now and then
snuck a peek.

Deano fetched me a canvas bucket of water from the creek, and I dug
out a bar of soap and washed myself off as best I could. While I was drying
off with another gunny sack and putting on my rig, I asked Deano if he'd
get another bucket for mama, and see if she'd like a handful of the calf
mix we'd brought, in a nose-bag. By then it was mid-afternoon, and felt
like we'd done a day's work already, so set up camp right here for the night.
I asked if either of the boys might want to cook, and Willy said sure, if

you'd point me the way, so he made up a fire while I unpacked the grill and Dutch oven.

By the time he had sausages browned, sliced up and stirred in with potatoes and onions and cheese and vegetables in the Dutch oven for a casserole, the two calves were on their feet and mama had started them nursing. Two baby heifers and their mama, all healthy and sound. I checked them all over and gave each a shot of a broad-spectrum antibiotic. Then decided we should watch them for the night, since we were so far from home. There were critters out here that might smell the milk and blood and come a-running. I dug out a windup alarm clock so we could keep watch, and the old .30-30 carbine from my saddle scabbard.

I made a pot of coffee, for the night watch. While we ate, Deano was silent, though Willy was suddenly full of belated questions. I told them these three animals represented quite a haul. The heifer had bred later than usual, probably from one of the bulls ranging free.

Are first births always hard?

Can be. It's really the shock and stress of the unknown for the young cow, as much as anything. After one birth, the cow's pelvis spreads a little, and it gets easier. You never want to pull too hard. Back at the barn we've got a stethoscope, thermometer, forceps and several kinds of pullers, but the kit we carry for these rides is pretty good, and has all you really need.

If you know what you're doing.

Yes, there is that. We try to time the breeding and insemination so the cows all come due the same time, while they're still in the big pens and easy to get to, before the spring drive. 283 days is the average, about nine and a half months. But this is one clever little heifer, She's been staying off the radar out here in the back country, making it all on her own, most likely. She might be ours or she might be one of our neighbors', but most likely nobody's. I can tell you one thing, it's lucky for her we come along when we did. That mountain lion woulda made quick work of her.

So what are we gonna do now?

I'm going to get some shut-eye, while one of you watches, set to wake me in four hours. Keep our little girl fed and watered, and let the babies as close as she wants 'em to be. If she wants to lay down, that's fine. Just stay as close as she'll let you.

Anything else?

Yeah. Talk to her a little, let her get used to your voice.

What'll we do in the morning?

We'll have to see. If the babies are fine, we can carry them a ways on the pommel in front of us wrapped in gunny sacks. If mama's up to it we might ride some fence, nice and slow, and stop whenever we need to. It's up to them, not us.

With that, I bade the boys good night, repeated the thought about waking me in four hours, that I would be taking the night watch.

The next thing I knew was a roar and a flash, a foot of flame out the muzzle of the .30-30. I jumped up with the flashlight in my hand and headed for the noise. It was Willy with the rifle across the clearing, sitting at the foot of a tree. Mama was bawling a little, so were the babies. Willy was talking to all three, calming them. I asked if he'd seen the big cat, and he said no, it was too dark, but it was close by, thrashing around. Somewhere between him and the ponies on the picket line. He figured the safest thing was just shoot straight up in the air. Deano seemed agitated, dazed, and wanted to know what to do. I said there was nothing to worry about, go back to sleep. Then I dug around in the supplies for the ziplock bag of mothballs we carried just in case, wandered off to sprinkle them around the horses and the calves, then relieved Willy and told him to get some rest. And that he did good, did just the right thing, and was set to make a real cowboy.

I watched the rest of the night, and let the boys sleep. At dawn, I stirred up the fire and made fresh coffee. While Willy was flipping three huge heaps of flapjacks, Deano pulled me aside to have a word. He said he didn't think he could do this job, that the calf births made him queasy at the sight of all that shit and blood. He said he'd just wanted to ride horses and have fun out of doors.

I guess I didn't really know what this was all about. I don't want to be shooting mountain lions, and standing guard over cows.

I see. Do you mind helping us out till we get home? Or would you rather find your own way back? I knew pretty much what the next couple days would bring, and what his answer would be, just wanted him to hear himself saying it. The first few days on most jobs never let you get this far

in. Besides, another couple days might just get him far enough from what
scared him, to give it another try.

Stumble-Step

If they had their druthers, most hands on the place would sit a tall horse and work cows. But there were always those who could farm if they had to, though they might grumble over the plowing and planting and weeding, coaxing things out of the ground, bucking bales. But as Len says, where else will winter hay and oats and feed corn come from—it don't grow on trees, and whatever you buy, you surrender the profit. There would always be a few mechanics, who could work and fix any manner of machine. The thing is, to run a big rambling operation like the K-Bar, the foreman Len Dawes needs it all to get done, not just what the boys care to tackle, so he keeps a little notebook in his vest pocket with a fat rubber band, that they know all about from a distance, watch him make notes with a stub of a pencil, and reckon who can do what, for whatever kind of project comes along. The K-Bar is one of those outfits that never hires a thing done, or throws a thing away. There's a complete blacksmith shop, with shoeing stocks and several barrels of shoes, with gas and arc welders, and a pile of ancient well drilling equipment all dismantled and stacked in a shed, that nobody remembers where it's from or how to get it up working again. Then too we have a row of old pickups in the weeds back of the shop where they can be fixed up or resurrected, or else picked through and plundered for parts, since every three or four years, depending, they buy another of the same exact make and model, which just makes good sense, to always have a spare transmission or A-frame or starter motor on hand when you need one, with that dealer a good hundred miles away.

With horses as with cattle, the K-Bar crew breeds, raises and trains their own replacements. Every year they fatten and sell the yearlings, keep a few head to butcher and eat on the place, and turn out a few of the likeliest heifers to add to the breed stock. The herd that has slowly built over time has gotten to be worth a second look, and same as guarantees us a future. And just like they bale their own hay, the boys pitch and spread manure, that also speaks to things getting better as they go.

In Len Dawes' little book he also keeps notes on what each of the boys did that month, not just what they're good at. If they work breaking and training horses they might get an H by their name, where some who ride and herd cattle never get more than an R. There are several that take a turn cooking to give Bixler the Cook a night off, get a C, and some that can work on motors, fix machinery, that might get an M. One or two might get a B for butchering and packaging a steer for the freezer. There are just a few that can do a little of everything—shoe horses, handle breeding, doctor sick calves. Climb up on the windmill and grease it, while the frame sways with your weight in a cold wind. One or two with a whole alphabet by their names might at last get a T, which that month might double their salary. These are top hands, leaders, few and far between.

We had one real farm boy out of Idaho, Clyde, who had grown up on an old-timey horse farm, that could do anything on the place. A black-smith who could hammer-weld broken parts, and a top-notch ferrier. He could make wine out of anything. He even baked bread on his Sundays off, three loaves that were always gone by sundown, before they got a chance to cool. Clyde's only shortcoming might have been that he threw spuds into everything he cooked, since they were what he knew and liked best. Plus he mostly liked to work alone.

Len never made a fuss about who did what, unless it was a dirty job he needed to motivate. And nobody would complain about the wages, which weren't all that much, but the grub was good and plenty, and the bunk-house roof didn't leak, at least not over anybody's bed. We all knew we had it better than what most of the hands got other places, so we kept our traps shut.

As for cowboying, for a while when you're young you have all the time in the world. You barely need to lay your head down for the night. Come time the sky lightens up, you're practically saddled and gone. Maybe cowboys share a little extra delusion since they call themselves boys to the end. Ride like the wind where it's mostly the horse with the hot blood and muscle, and them astride, holding on for as long as they can.

But then comes the day when you tip your head back and look out from under your hat brim, out to where the wide sky touches down, and realize you can see further than you might ever ride again. That you need to ask what you want to do right now, and do mostly that while there's time.

If you want to shingle a roof, best get up the ladder while you can. So these days Len Dawes was starting to think of stepping down.

He made no announcements. And the boys had no idea what retirement for Len Dawes might even look like. He'd always been silent as the grave about himself, and being foreman kept him a loner, as it mostly will. He had bought a little piece of ground of his own, 40 acres with a house he'd knocked together by himself, hiring a few of the boys on their days off to help mix and pour concrete, tip up walls, toenail rafters and such, all that three- and four-handed work. But he did everything he could by himself, and the boys he hired said it was good and solid, built to last. So what was he going to do, start a ladies' riding academy? His place was too far out from town.

But then there come a hitch, as will happen to the best and worst. One day when we were off doctoring some cows he took a spill—or rather, his horse Strongbow put a foot wrong. But then down he went. They said it only took a minute, but then Len got up slow and checked the big dun horse over before he got back on. I didn't see how it went, since I was off looking for the other cow that needed a shot, that was holed up in a thicket, practically had to be dug out of there with a pitchfork.

But that night after supper Len pulls me aside for a talk. We go out the barn to the back of the tack room that he makes do for an office. He sets a little fire in the potbelly stove to take off the chill, lights an Aladdin lamp, then settles into an old armchair, and reaches down to pet his dog sprawled on the floor. Boney is an old cow dog that's always been great on the drives. Boney, short for Bonaparte, works about as good as any mounted hand to turn the herd.

He starts off saying, You know, I can tell how a hand feels about the job and himself just by how his hat sets on his head. Practically says who you are.

Yeah?

I notice you practically always wear your big old black hat. You wouldn't change it to set the points on your pickup. You wear it the same mending fence. Or catching a green horse.

What do you figure that means?

He says Something, though who's to say. It's always been clear to me you weren't born to the life. You had to go learn for yourself, like I did. But back somewhere you must of had horse people, everybody did, and farming folks, so it would be there in your blood come the need.

I study that a minute. Tell Len I had a female second cousin who kept chickens and knew her way around wild mushrooms, showed me a thing or two. Then I say You got an awful good dog there. Did you train each other, or did he raise you up from a pup?

That's how he was when I got him. Sometimes you get lucky.

I've heard you tell the boys there's no such thing as luck.

Probably speaking of gambling. Never pays to gamble. But sometimes cowboyin' is all luck, nothing but. Just don't tell 'em I said that.

We talk horses a while. Len says Ol' Strongbow is still the best I ever had, so far as that goes. I could ride Bow half a day with not much more than my knees. Turn my head and he looks to go that way. When I want him to pull up I lift the reins with a couple fingers off his neck, and he stops. That's a horse. You had that Apache that would still be going strong, if he hadn't stepped on that power line that come down in a snowstorm. We thought the power was out all over, didn't know.

I tell Len I had a thought the other night when I couldn't sleep. That maybe Apache thought that power line was a snake, sparking in the snow, and was trying to kill it. I recall how he once killed a big timber rattler in camp, pounced on it before I even noticed. Even so, we agree it was a hard way to go. He was a good horse. The way he worked cattle he same as read their minds.

But you know, now, my Strongbow just got old.

I heard today, all it was, he put a foot wrong.

Just between us he's startin' to stumble a little. Like he's tired. But I wouldn't want that getting around. Your Apache was a year or two older and still just as sharp as they come. Tell me, were you taking it easy on him? Holding back any?

Not so's you'd notice.

I thought not. Some horses go on into their mid-late twenties. But there always comes a day.

Yeah.

Which is a goddamn shame. With that Len heaves up and reaches into the bottom desk drawer. Says You know I'm no drinkin' man, but there's a time and a place for everything. Could you use a snort, Ben?

I expect I could. We're done for the evening.

Len comes up with a dusty bottle he keeps there, and a couple glasses, which is, to hear Len tell it, strictly medicinal. We each get a good splash, and ring them together as he says To all the good horses and women, plus a couple of each that are wicked.

Then we taste the whiskey, study it in the dim light, feel the burn going down.

I think Strongbow same as told me today he's about done with me.

He's a tall horse, is all. It's a good ways to the ground.

I didn't break nothing, but I coulda. Layin' there I rolled my head lookin' around for my hat, and noticed a boulder alongside me the size of a dump truck, that coulda finished me.

There's always close calls, Len, always will be. You know that. So here's to near misses, which are the best lookin' kind. We raise our glasses and drink to that, and sit quiet a minute.

What I mean, Ben, it got my attention. I got Bow up on his feet, but come time we rode in, he was limping. I got down to take the load off, and let him walk that last mile, and damn if I wasn't half-limpin' myself.

Like they say, It'll feel better in the morning, and look worse. Think you could spare another splash a that—what d'you call it?

Medicinal.

I reach for the bottle and splash us each some more.

Well, here, let this seep in your bones and see don't it soften the hard knocks a little.

We lift and touch our glasses, then sip. Len says I really wanted to have your thoughts about a couple things.

Like what?

What do you think I should do?

Hell, I don't know. You seriously thinking a quitting us?

It's occurred to me lately.

Look, Len. You're good at it, in a way most people ain't. The Kendricks family, ol' Lionel and his little sister Lucille, they got no notion how damn good you are. You make it look easy, right where it's anything but.

Len considers that a minute. Then he says Maybe it's just the bottle talkin', but I'm about done giving orders. Tired a the thinkin' ahead an' the plannin', all that. Think I might find me a sweet little widow woman, and settle for the ride.

He looks up and over at me, says How does that strike you?

Sounds pretty damn good. But then what do I know? Never had much success with the ladies.

I know how that is. But it could change.

Maybe you could use a younger horse. You could run a little spread, and make a go. That piece you got is not so far from some federal grazing lands. You could sign up and run you some cows.

I could.

Besides, you might wake up tomorrow full a beans, and go scoutin' that new horse. I'd be glad to help.

Len shakes his head, turns and looks right at me. Ben, he says, What do you see up ahead for yourself?

I'm not fillin' your shoes. You got a dozen years on me, and I ain't half the man.

You're a top hand, Ben, the best we got. You got the smarts. You could ramrod this outfit.

Ol' Lionel might just want to get him a new broom, and clean house.

He might. But to start with, he'll do what I tell him, which means you'll get your chance.

Len, face it. Lionel Kendricks don't know I'm alive.

Well, you stick around, he soon will. When we come out to your place for that party for the Birdsalls, it was all he could talk about for a month.

That's kind of you to say.

Just makes sense. So think about it, will you. Tomorrow maybe we can look around for that young horse, and put ol' Strongbow out to pasture with a few old-timers, and see how he bounces back.

One more toast, Len.

All right.

There's never a horse that couldn't be rode

And never a cowboy that couldn't be throwed.

We both laugh, and Len says Now ain't that the truth.

A couple days later Len looks me up after breakfast, says We've got an invite to dinner tonight, up at the big house.

You sure about this?

All I done was put your name in the hat. You're the one'll have to do the work. So quit your worryin'. Look here, they promoted me up off the place. May a been pure laziness, but I've never heard a complaint. Their daddy ol' Gander Kendricks was a real cowboy. Far as that goes, so was his daddy before him. That's why they picked me, and I think that's still what they want. And it ain't hard to see that's what you are, no mistake. Just be straight with 'em, and tell yourself if they're partial to cowboys, you're it. Otherwise, they're idjits.

So I scrape off the dirt and whiskers, put on my Sunday best, and catch up with Len in the barn and walk with him up the hill in the twilight as the mourning doves start to call from the grove down by the creek, and the swallows swoop low after bugs.

There is Lionel holding forth in front of the big fireplace in the living room, with cedar kindling snapping and popping against the screen. His sister Lucille and her husband Anthony Depew the accountant look skinny and frail in a couple of overstuffed leather chairs. Then there is the lawyer and family friend Archie Mayhew, leaning on the mantle with his silver mane. Len leads me to Lionel, who shakes my hand, then makes introductions all around. I sense there are three parties here, maybe even three and a half. Lionel makes one, independent and unpredictable but in charge. His sister Lucille is another, both of them with agendas that reach back most of their lives. And then there are the retainers, of which Len Dawes is still one, and the most grounded as head of the day-to-day workings of the ranch, though Lucille's husband Anthony does the ranch's taxes and books, and Archie Mayhew handles all legal matters and administers the family trust, so between them hold legal and fiduciary sway. Out of the blue I remember Lucille and Anthony's boys, and ask after Max and Tony Junior. It turns out they're both upstairs doing homework and watching TV.

And it turns out they all recognize me, clear back to when I was on the spot when Gander Kendricks had his massive heart attack. Though I was still a boy I had helped carry him to the truck and lay him on the back seat, then rode in with Len to unload him at the hospital in town.

Lionel offers me something to drink, and I take a cold Dos Equis. Then they all want to hear what they call my story, which to them means family. I say there's not much to tell, then lay out what little there is, about my father Randy Wilder a farm boy from outside Merced running an auto body shop in Fresno till the day of my eleventh birthday, when his car got hit by a train at a grade crossing. Faulty signal arm that never blinked or rang the bell or come down to stop him. With a new bike for me in the trunk, that got crushed with the box it came in. The day after his funeral me and my younger sister and brother got farmed out to relatives while Mom went looking for another man. Which I gather she never found before her end. How I ended up in San Angelo, Texas, with Clyde Hooper and his wife Mayellen, who was actually my mom's cousin so my second cousin, but still a pretty good egg. But Clyde taken a belt to me when I was 17, come in late from a school dance with beer on my breath, and I had hit him with a tub full of dirty dishes it was my job to wash, grabbed my coat and lit out right there in the middle of the night. Slept under some bushes out at the west end of town, and over the next couple days I walked the roads, hitchhiked around scoutin' work. And got lucky, hired on as kitchen helper at a ranch, the Lazy B. I'd already learned a little cooking from Mayellen, who kept chickens and showed me how to hunt wild mushrooms. I could chop and peel like a demon, caught on quick and was never scared of work. Pretty soon they had me going on a drive as chuck wagon cook. Along the way I learned riding and roping and driving their team of mules as I went.

So how come you're not still on the Lazy B? Lionel is nothing if not direct.

They needed a cook too bad to let me try anything else.

Sounds like you tried it all anyhow. What kind of a cook were you?

Fair to middling. I know to taste what I'm cooking. But the hands wanted it all plain vanilla, where I kept wanting to fool around, spice it up a little.

So you didn't last?

I trained my first horse in the hours I had off between meals. That next season I moved on, and at the Rockin' R Ranch didn't mention kitchen work at all. Told 'em I was fit to make a top hand some day, though I still had to borrow a saddle. Worked that place two years, and wore out the old one they lent me.

And why'd you leave there?

Tell you the truth, I'd heard about the K-Bar. Liked what I heard, so I gave my notice and come out to give you a try.

You quit that other job, before you even laid eyes on this place?

Yessir.

Lotta confidence for a youngster. What exactly did you hear?

Mostly little things. That you had a good ramrod, for one. All the boys knew about Len, that he was calm and fair, and said what he thought. Heard your horses were fine. And mostly how the grub was good.

Everybody laughed.

It may have been all rumors an' dumb luck, but I found what I was looking for.

How long you been here now?

Goin' on thirty-two years.

With that Lionel looks over at Len, then turns to me and says I'd like to hear your thoughts about any changes to the place. When I give Len the eye, he tips back his head and looks away, as if to let me know I'm on my own, so don't go so far out on a limb I can't get myself back.

I say I been around long enough to figure out why some things are done like they are, but not everything. So maybe it's too soon for changes. How about if I tell you a few things I like about the K-Bar, that should never change.

All right.

Well, first thing is how you don't have the whole place covered in roads. Old State Route 6 works just fine for trucking livestock to market. The trails you got take a little upkeep, but not a thing like roads. It's the trails that keep the place working horses, which is how it ought to be.

Why is that?

You've seen places that work their cattle with those stinkpot ATVs. Keeps the livestock nervous, all stirred up. Don't gain weight so easy, I suspect.

And with that, one of the kitchen help steps in to announce dinner is served. When Lucille and Anthony's two boys come down from upstairs, they step up, say their names and shake my hand, then we all go in and sit down. Here come platters of steaks and steamed vegetables and baked potatoes and whatnot, and they uncork a couple bottles of wine to pass around. Then for a little while it's just like the boys in the bunk house—no more talk, just the serious sounds of eating, china and cutlery and such.

After dinner we go back out to the fireplace in the big hall. Lucille, that only her brother calls Lucy, approaches me and asks what I know about their mother Eleanor. I say I remember her and her taste in clothes and fancy things. And her carriage, how straight she held herself, though she got thin as a rail in the years that I knew her.

What do you figure she thought of this place?

I didn't get to see her all that much, but expect she cared about it a good deal.

Why is that?

She knew most of the livestock by name, and seemed to watch over them. Last time we talked she asked after Dockerty, our old kitchen mule.

The last twenty years of her life she lived in that downstairs front room in the oldest part of the house, Lucille says, pointing across the hall. Kept her binoculars right there on the window sill.

She was from back East, wasn't she?

Yes, but it's not what you'd expect. There is something in Lucille's tone of voice that quiets the others, who had been talking about how different breeds of cattle stand the heat. How spreads like the K-Bar cross Hereford cows with Charlevois and Brahma bulls. She says Eleanor grew up on a farm in New Hampshire, that had a regular dairy herd. Did you ever hear any stories about when she was a child?

I shake my head. The others are listening intently.

Eleanor could just barely walk when she started following the milk cows round the pasture. It was hard to keep her from doing it, or even keep track of her once she could work a doorknob. So this one muddy spring morning she was out following the cows when she stumbled and fell face-down in a drainage ditch and got stuck. Well, their oldest smartest cow Hulga had been watching. She came over and bent down and worked one of her horns up under the straps on the baby's overalls, and picked her up in the air. There that muddy little girl was, hanging up on the side of old Hulga's head, blinking, not making a sound. Then the old cow turned around and plodded back to the barnyard, and stood by the fence with all the other cows around, till somebody noticed them. That limp little baby girl all covered in mud hanging there never cried or squirmed or anything. Finally her mama happened to look out from the house, and came rushing out onto the porch, followed by all the rest. Then they all got quiet, and whispered to each other back and forth. You know what they were saying, Ben?

Who knew and liked that old cow the best.

Exactly. Then their old hand, Virgil, who did most of the milking, walked out to the fence, climbed over and talked to Hulga a little, un-hooked the baby and lifted her down.

Lionel came over to Lucille, and said Lucy, where'd you hear all that?

From Eleanor, on one of her shopping trips. We'd have lunch when she'd come to the city.

How come I never heard that one?

She didn't think it was something to be proud of. She said she didn't remember all that much, just the mud in her eyes and nose, and the taste of it in her mouth. But her mama and old Virgil told her all about it, plus a couple of the older kids who'd been there.

I bet she felt that bond with animals her whole life.

Lucille looks up at me, nods and smiles.

Then Lionel says I think we've about heard enough, and these boys likely need their rest. Len Dawes laughs, then everyone eases out onto the porch to shake hands and see us off.

They all wave and watch us go, then turn back inside.

As we crunch along in the dark on the gravel, I ask Len how he thought it went. He says I think that old lady from beyond the grave same as picked you out herself.

The First Knowing and the Last

Twice a year at spring and fall roundups, for a few days the boys scour these bland, forgettable hills that seem to roll away forever all the same. Easy to get lost in, hard to find a cow. This is the time to locate the herd, stir it up and drive it in, see what we got, sort through and take what is set to be taken to market, good as it's likely to get. There are places never seen the whole rest of the year, trails who knew what first made on what errand or whim. Now come the nights around the fire, dog-tired but stirred up and poked for the sparks trailing up the night sky. Here come stories about the times out here because it matters, it's who and what we are, without the books and bright lights, TV and radio, smart phone apps and the rest that stand in for human knowing. Sometimes the mind at work needs to feel on the loose yet on top of things, roaming at large on the spread, deeds given fresh life in the telling, since doing is still the first knowing and will likely be the last.

So we hear-tell stories of the traces and trails, the game runs and roaming wagon roads. The Natchez Trace and the Santa Fe Trail before even the Oregon Trail. And then too the great cattle drives on the Goodnight-Loving Trail and the Chisholm Trail and the rest. These nights the talk has a life of its own, feels sometimes like secrets saved up till some shining moment lit to pass on like a torch, told poker-faced, just lively and silly enough for a story stretched beyond living memory, meant to last. Who rode together, till their riding stopped. What they found or built. What great horses were turned out to pasture, let run wild their final years, nothing more, nothing less.

Maybe in an excess of spirits thinking ahead to the rodeo circuit, the boys would sometimes compete to see who had the best cutting horse. But that's where the stories came in. Actual horses and cows on the loose in rough country never stood a chance against the old foreman, Len Dawes, who was still around to tell you he used to have a mare, Dixon, that never tasted bit nor bridle, only halter or hackamore, who could herd a whole flock of chickens set loose in a field and from the herd cut out a single hen.

Once he showed the mare which one he wanted, Len could ease down out of his stirrups, loop her reins over the saddle horn and she would circle the flock and drive the one chicken straight home to him. He used to say if he ever got tired of cattle she might run sheep or field mice or bumblebees or any other damn thing worth her attention. As a kid new to the place I'd met Dixon, when she was a swayback gone gray in the muzzle, and have to say she still had a thing about chickens. They seemed to do what she wanted, and she still enjoyed pleasing Len Dawes.

It had struck me long ago that the young ones didn't just want to hear about the past, they wanted to hear about the past in the present, that old stuff still around and alive. Like the hitching rail by the bunk house, and the identical one by the big house, a hundred years old if they're a day, that stand for something even in the dark with nothing tied there, that meant here were hands that still used horses to herd cattle and get the work done.

But since I took over running the show, this roundup Len and I thought about doing something different, maybe lead the talk in a different direction, around the long way home. He said The stories we need to hear grow out of the work of the day. And it always helps to have a few new hands along, green as grass, like calves and heifers staring hard at you, skeptical and mute, trying to make sense of everything while they got a minute. So he said What if you start off by asking the youngest and the oldest hands to tell their stories first. And we happened to be in luck, on account of who that meant.

The newest hand was Casey Pratt. When I called his name he snatched a long forked stick out of the fire with a couple tongues of flame at one end, waved it back and forth a couple times like he wasn't sure if it wanted to burn or blow out. When we were quiet he says I'm Casey Pratt, and I was no cowboy to start with. Have to say I come of a good family, middle of three, mama's a nurse and dad's an accountant. Got into college figuring to do some kinda science, but kept changing courses then majors. Starting out it felt like I wanted to know it all so studied hard, but one dark night saw I didn't want to spend the rest of my days tied to a desk, and couldn't find anything I still wanted to know all that bad, besides what I could do with my two hands. Decided I needed to work at something real for a change.

So I answered an ad for a job working for a corporation that raised and processed cattle. I drove an ATV around, if you can believe it, through this big maze of feedlots and pens. There was no range to speak of, and not much grass anywhere. They told us the land was worth too much to waste grazing cattle. Better to pump the water, grow alfalfa, corn and soybeans, grind and feed that. So that's what we did. It was a 24-7 operation with someone on duty to keep the feed and water coming round the clock. They had a little herd of maybe a dozen cows with their calves, on what would have been the lawn out front of the main buildings, with a split rail fence and a big log entrance for show. That's what had first caught my eye, those mamas and babies that all seemed so peaceful and healthy and calm. But the real business back behind the big buildings was noisy bare dirt smelly enough to gag a goat when the wind blew wrong. The corporation looked to buy calves at around two hundred pounds, feed 'em up to a thousand, then process 'em. They never said the word slaughter. The corporation shipped out packaged frozen meats to another corporation they'd bought, with a fleet of reefer trucks that supplied restaurants and hotel chains, hospitals, prisons, nursing homes and whatnot all over the country.

So there I am. After a few months I know I can't stand the job, though there's something about it I do like. When I sit down to figure out what, I see it must be the animals. Especially those nice contented ones eating grass for show, out front of the office complex. There was something there you couldn't fake. I checked those cows and calves against the thousands we had in the feed lots, and thought at least we weren't painting grins on their faces.

Then one day a bean counter comes around to give us a talk on what it takes to make a cow happy in dollars and cents, so we'll all understand how the place turns a profit, and when he's done I go into the office and give my notice. Then I climbed into my old car and headed south and west, looking for work on a real ranch, with real horses, and cattle that eat grass like they're 'sposed to. I know, that makes me a dreamer and a fool and not much else. So it took a little looking around three or four states, till I finally got a tip from a fella camped up at tree line above Farley, New Mexico, that steered me to this place. I was up there for the view, but even a fool can get lucky. So I finally found my way. And I have to say you gave me a chance here at something I wasn't all that familiar with. And were patient with me till I caught on what this place is up to, what the life is about. And for that I thank you. I'd love to have a place of my own some day, but what with the stretch between wages and land prices that ain't likely. So for now I'll curry my pony, and keep oilin' my saddle, and got no more to say.

There was a murmur of assent that quickly flared and died. Casey tossed his forked stick back in the fire and sat down.

Then the oldest hand on the place, Mebbee Jones, hobbled into the firelight. Up in his eighties somewhere, not even he could say how old he was. Nobody knew why he was called Mebbee, and he never said, just told his name, and nobody on the K-Bar thought a thing or said a word. Mebbee never was known to talk much, so when I asked him to speak up, everybody got quiet.

He said Mine ain't much of a story. My folks got caught in the Dust Bowl out in Okema, Oklahoma, a little before my time, when the sky went black for days, and all the good in their land blew away. I was born in one of those camps along the road west. Coulda been Texas, New Mexico, Arizony, Nevada. Even Californy. Never had no birth certificate, mama wasn't rightly sure just where or how to apply, and we had no money to spare on what she called pedigrees. She said she was scared I was a-coming, then all at once here I was. And I woke up late, didn't learn what hard times even meant till they was practically done. Mama would boil up a ripe ear of corn, cut the kernels off, crush and strain the corn milk to give us young ones to drink, and I still recollect the taste, that wasn't half-bad. I missed the big war since I wasn't but eleven when it ended, those two A-bombs dropped on Japan. My people were country people, what they called Okies, that knew to work horses and plow land till the sky turned black with it. Out in Californy they picked and worked crops, but never did quite get back to farming a place of their own. They never had all that much, and whatall they had went straight to the bank or perdition. My dad Chauncey and my uncle Edward found a horse ranch up in the canyons north of L.A., that was owned by some old silent movie star, and they got on as horse wranglers. And soon as I was big enough to sit a tall horse, along about fourteen, they got me on there too.

It wasn't a bad life, workin' horses. The place paid its keep as kind of a dude ranch for friends of the old movie star. I'd likely still be there if it was still in business. But all of a sudden the place got taken and sold for back taxes, that the old movie star hadn't paid in forever. And there we was out on our ear. The boss man said we could each have a horse instead of that final paycheck, which was a laugh, since what were we 'sposed to feed it. The boys joked about how you get to love the taste of horse meat after the third day of nothin'—but not this boy.

I picked me out a good strong blackfaced young gelding that was still half a baby, so fresh he'd never been rode, climbed aboard and pretty quick we reached an understanding, then next morning lit out on horseback headed east. This was before the freeways, so it wasn't bad. The world was still empty then, mostly quiet. I had a rope and a saddle, a bean pot and a couple blankets, and thought I was set to go places. It was early spring, but up in the passes it was winter yet, and every now and then it would sleet or snow to where you couldn't see your hand in front of your face, and there was nothin' to burn to keep warm.

And here I was on my own heading east, no more than sixteen years old, with nobody and nothing around but that young horse. When we started out he didn't even have a name. That first night I got down off the road, and camped in the dark in a dry gulch under a bridge. I didn't really even know why I was heading east. Never mind Okema, I had nobody back anywhere I knew to so much as say howdy. I hadn't been getting along with my folks for a while, and had been bunking in the hayloft at the ranch. The folks were struggling themselves, with not a mouthful to spare. My two older brothers and sister were long gone, drifted off after jobs and lovers and whatnot. The factory work had started up with the war, making airplanes and ships and bombs and uniforms, but then those jobs went away. For us Okies it was like the Depression took a time-out, never quit for good.

It was a week or two till I woke up wonderin' what I was doin' out here eatin' nothin' but beans in a pot. I snuck through Needles and Kingman and Flagstaff in the night. It gradually dawned on me I was trying to find where I come from, what I was made of, scouting a spot that would look and feel like home. A start. That wasn't Oklahoma for me, never had been, since I'd never seen it, and this home I dreamt of was no more than a shady spot on the road. I knew I was born on the move and had never stopped till

I lost that first job. So in time I come to see my home was the road itself, where I was from and grew up. And a couple weeks out there jabberin' to myself an' that colt made me the man I still am.

That was when my little horse kinda grew up too. He wasn't just a ride, he was the answer to every question I could think to ask, since he was stronger than me, and I was bound to go where he'd take me. For that first few weeks he was never out of my sight, and I mostly gave him his head. Since I wasn't sure of anything, I'd say Mebbee we'll get there by dark. Mebbee there'll be water fit to drink. I started calling him Mebbee, and it stuck.

Then one night up in the mountains my luck changed. I had found a scrap of canvas to roll my blankets in, that kept me warm, and had whittled a pair of hobbles for Mebbee, out of some wood and a piece of tire chain I found by the roadside, so he wouldn't wander off while I slept. But this night whenever I dozed off, Mebbee kept wakin' me, snorting in the dark, stamping and shivering and whinnying. At first I thought it was the cold, and finally he was standing right up against me, so close I could feel that horse shake. We had no light, just the box of matches in my pocket. I reached out and petted his front legs, that had the hobbles on, and said What's the matter, boy? Just then something snarled and jumped on his back, and he reared up and bolted, just kinda hopping, since he couldn't run. It was a mountain lion, a big old thing that musta been hungry as we were. I kicked out of the blankets and snatched up a big stick of wood from the fire that was still smoldering on the other end. I shouted and swung at that lion and hit him hard a couple times. Knocked him off the horse's neck and kicked him away. He made a fuss but I kept after him and drove him off. I don't know what I was thinking, tackling a cat that was bigger than I was. And me barefoot. But without Mebbee I knew I was done anyhow. And I was so groggy I didn't stop to think or nothing, just waded into that cat in the dark till it was gone.

We were both shakin' pretty bad. I built the fire up, and looked the horse over. He was bit and scratched pretty good on his neck and back, and I had no medicine. Not so much as a bar of soap or a warshrag. It was a whole day back to the last town, twenty-four miles by the last road sign. I had all of two dollars and thirty-four cents and a sack of dry beans. So I got some water and washed out his wounds, then gave him a drink, took those hobbles and threw 'em across the road into the far ditch, shook out my rope and tied him to a shattered old juniper tree. He could run sixty feet if the lion came back, so at least had him a fighting chance.

He never left my side for the rest of that night, his front hooves tucked up against my back. I felt bad about those hobbles, wondered what the hell was I thinkin'. By first light Mebbee wasn't bleeding but his wounds looked worse, puffy and angry, so I saddled up and pushed on east, hoping to find a town, at least a turnoff where there might be folks with some idée how to doctor him.

In the middle of that afternoon on a long uphill climb there was a hand-painted sign that said Harper, and I turned off to the south, stepped down from the saddle and led Mebbee on these gravel ruts up into the hills. He was starting to stumble and breathe hard, and he hadn't had much to eat all day. Every couple hundred steps we had to stop and rest. Several miles into rough country the track ended in a clearing at a cabin handmade of rough timbers and stone. I led Mebbee to the door and knocked, and in a few minutes a bearded man with long grizzled hair came out. He was tall and lean, and a little stooped, but with eyes that were fierce and bright. I introduced myself and asked if this was Harper. He laughed and said it wasn't a place but a man, and patted his own chest. I told how the mountain lion come in the night, and asked if he knew about doctoring animals. He shook his head, said he wished he did, and had a look at Mebbee's scratches and bites. Right away he said let's get that saddle and blanket off, and he went inside while I loosened the cinch and heaved it down by his doorstep. Harper came back with a bottle of whiskey and a bucket of water, that Mebbee drank nonstop till it was gone. He said the alcohol will help clean out the horse's wounds, but you better do it, since it's gonna sting, and he'll probably let you do it easier than me. When that's done we'll try this bar of soap.

He had a quick and friendly way that gave me confidence. I cleaned Mebbee's wounds with a rag dipped in the whiskey, that made him shake all over like I'd given him a bath. Then I got some more water and lathered up the soap. I asked Mr. Harper if he had anything that a horse might eat, and he went in and got a round box of rolled oats, that I fed Mebbee a little

at a time out of my open hand. He also had a carrot and a couple of apples
that looked a little wrinkled, that the horse liked better than anything he'd
seen in weeks. Mr. Harper stood there looking at the horse, said some of
those wounds were pretty deep, but looks like he's got a chance. Then he
went around and pulled his old Model T out of the shed and said we should
put Mebbee in here for the night. He got a scythe down from the shed
rafters and took long slow swipes at what was left of his yard, for some hay
for the horse. When we'd bundled it in and spread it out over the concrete,
he filled his water bucket again and I led the horse in. Harper said At least
it'll keep the wind off him.

It was getting dark by the time we went inside and ate—a leftover stew
and some grilled cheese sandwiches that tasted like heaven. We talked a
good while. Turned out Harper was some kind of a professor, up here by
himself to write a book about the first atom bomb. He said it was a silent
flash that seemed to stop time, that someone said was like a thousand suns.
He'd seen that first one at White Sands when he was in the Army, standing in a trench facing it, with special smoked glasses and a paper mask over
his mouth. When I asked what he thought, Harper said It purely scared
hell out of me. So much bigger and more powerful and dangerous than any
such thing ought to be. Some generals and politicians said it could mean
the end of war, since there would be no answering it. But some said this
might be the end of life as we know it. Some even thought it might trigger a
chain reaction that would blow up the planet. But then they laughed at the
nervous nellies and shot it off anyhow.

While I did the dishes, Harper started to make me a bed on the couch.
I thanked him but said I needed to go sleep with the horse, he'd be calmer
that way. He nodded, and I grabbed up my bedroll and headed out into the
night.

When I cracked the doors and peeked into the shed I didn't see the
horse, and thought he had got out. But he was down, and having trouble
breathing. I went back to tell Harper, but there was nothing to be done. I
spent the night with his head in my lap, and Mebbee died about sunup.

So Mr. Harper helped me drag him out in the sun and bury him.
When that was done we said some words, and I took that horse's name and
the loan of ten dollars that took me a year to pay back. Then Mr. Harper

gave me a ride into town with my saddle, and I hung out my thumb east of town and went on. 'Cause I knew already by then how the living don't stop for a minute. And wandered twenty years, all over the Southwest, took all manner of jobs working horses and cattle. But I was so restless that none of the jobs really took, till I got to that big bend in the river eight miles from here, with that old camping spot that something in me said was home, or near enough to finally settle for, and stop myself.

Against the Spin of the World

The K-Bar spread had never had a woman cook even in the big house, till Lionel Kendricks brought his stylish new ashen-blonde bride home from back East, with her jodhpurs and polished knee-high boots, her tight red hunting jacket, pancake English saddle and fuzzy black hard hat. Maybe to signal a changing of the guard, the dawn of a gentler era, Cynthia Mayweather Kendricks got to hire a new cook, which entailed a double surprise. Although Rosa's English was a bit hesitant, her dark eyes watched and signaled a deft and sure understanding. A sturdy shapely woman with a cheery manner and touches of gray in her hair, Rosa's cooking seemed effortless. She had a heartwarming way with spices, and her blend of border Tex-Mex and Indian cuisine was both stirring and comforting. She promptly took hold of the kitchen, and ran it as her own. With anyone asked to breakfast or supper on the spur of the moment, she was quick to set another place, offer coffee, a drink or iced tea. The other surprise arrived a week later, in the form of her daughter Estelle.

As ramrod I knew it was only a matter of time. I had seen women at rodeo events who could handle anything around a horse or cow a man could, short of lifting the injured beast on her shoulder to carry home. They just didn't crave winning belt buckles half as bad as the men. And now here was Estelle. The boys told me she approached the bunkhouse that first morning, to ask could she borrow a horse. They said she was dressed just like they were, in jeans with scuffed boots, a flannel shirt and vest, a wide hat and neckerchief, and leather work gloves in one hip pocket. It took a few minutes to understood she didn't really just want the loan of a horse for the morning. When they realized who she was and where she bunked, a couple of the boys volunteered to walk her around the big corral and show her which horses were and weren't spoken for. She had clearly learned from her mother to watch Anglos closely, how they answered as she pointed to one horse then another. Them two are part of Pete's string, one might say, or that's Davey's number one pony Blister. She took a step back and watched them both, sussing out signals and body language, sharp as a runner on second base stealing the catcher's signals.

Finally she pointed to one that hadn't been spoken for, which meant it was likely a wild one never ridden, used to avoiding attention, flowing with the herd. A rangy liver-colored young gelding with a ragged star on his forehead. When she clicked her tongue the young horse picked up his head. So she sidled alongside, stroked his shoulder and neck, offered a hand to his nose, then walked around him while she talked to him quietly, touched him all over, studying his feet and legs, his barrel and chest and hindquarters. There must have been something she liked, because when she got back to the others she had only one question: Does he have a name? The answer? Not so as anybody knows.

So she fed him the bit and buckled the throat latch on the bridle smooth as pie, then led him around, and he followed free and easy. She said she was taking the horse for a get-acquainted walk, went through the big gate out onto the open range, and was soon out of sight in the scrub and hills. She wasn't back till Cooky was clanging the iron rim on the porch of the cook shack for supper, and here she came riding the horse bareback, not leading him. Whatever she had done, there wasn't a mark on the gelding nor on her, and she had the horse's complete attention. Ears up, alert and confident. She slid down, led him into the big corral, checked him all over, curried, brushed and petted him, then slipped off his bridle and set him free. Estelle told the loafers gathered there his name was Bromistar— Joker. When one of the boys wondered why, she gave a little smile and said, Because he makes me laugh. Then she waved, and in the gathering dark walked up the drive to the big house.

I hadn't yet laid eyes on Estelle, having gone to town early, spent most of what would be her first day running errands and ordering supplies. But I got an earful of the house cook's daughter while I had a late supper of chicken enchiladas Bixler our Cooky had been keeping warm. The younger boys were mighty curious, and the two who had showed her around, Russ and Pedro, had a proprietary air, talking about her skill with horses, which they hadn't really seen, though what they said might count as pretty fair hearsay.

Sure, the hands thought they knew all about broke horses, and green-broke horses, and those that had never felt a rope or bit. Being broke was mostly a deal the horse made with you, some easier than others. If you quit riding them, they got harder to ride till eventually you were back where you started, having to catch and subdue an animal who was far from curious, intent on just running away. Nobody could blame them, and there were only a few tricks—what else but patience to calm their fears, touches and treats to reward their curiosity, and for their ears a nonsense lullaby. It was either that or the hard old way, the rope and snubbing post in the round pen, getting a saddle on and riding the fight out of them.

While I ate, Russ and Pedro recited their details back and forth, how Estelle knew right away not to pick anybody else's horse, how she looked that horse over pretty good, so had been looking for something but they couldn't tell what, in this Bromistar. As Pedro said in finale, So she has likely got an eye.

Then they quieted, waiting for me to say something, watching me fold a final tortilla to mop up the last of my plate. All I could say was You boys got the advantage of me. If she's half as good as you say, I'll have to look into this Estelle. Then I got up, washed my plate, and went out to the big corral to see could I find that horse in the twilight, but it was already too dark. All I saw was his star rising as the colt turned and shuffled away.

First thing next morning I did get a look at Bromistar, saw he was well put together, had a nice easy motion, on my way to the kitchen up at the big house. I knocked gently at the back door, said Buenos Dias to Rosa and begged a cup of coffee por favor. Rosa pointed to the pot, the cups upside down on a towel. She was in the middle of stirring eggs in her biggest skillet, practically a yard across, so I let her be till she had scooped the eggs into a serving dish, covered them with cheese and salsa and a lid, and carried them through the swinging door into the dining room. When she returned she smiled, said Buenos Dias, and sat down at the kitchen table. She already knew me, knew what I did on the place, folded her hands and held a comfortable silence. Then she raised her eyes.

It's about your daughter, Estelle.

Si?

She has done nothing, is in no trouble.

Si.

I just wanted to talk with you about her plans, her schooling, that kind of thing.

You must ask her.

Of course. But it would help if I knew your wishes.

That is very kind of you, Señor Ben. What is it you wish to know?

I shrugged. Rosa looked down at her hands, wiped them on her apron. Then she said Estelle was one of those never easy with school. Bright, but I don't know how she graduated this past spring. I don't know what it could be. Something may have happened that I never got to hear. She may have lacked interest. She may have lacked guidance. She never met her father. He was never in her life.

Is anyone in your family a vaquero?

There is her uncle, my older brother Eduardo. He works on a place outside San Angelo.

Is that where your daughter learned to work horses?

There was a slight noise, and Rosa picked up her head. A dark-haired young woman stood at the foot of the back stairs. Rosa said You must ask her. Estelle, this is Señor Ben Wilder, who manages the ranch.

She stepped forward, looked me in the eye and shook my hand. She said Buenos Dias. What do they call you?

Mostly Ben. Or some go with Boss.

Estelle was in her late teens, tall, smart, strong, and easy on the eyes. She dressed and moved right, fit the boys' description, and I could see how she might hold their attention. She pointed her long straight nose at whatever stirred her, and she wasn't shy. A metal box of some kind had worn its pale outline in one hip pocket of her jeans. She wore her hair in a shining dark braid down her back, that when she talked switched gently to and fro. She had her mother's fierce dark eyes, that could be mild one minute then flare up the next. Like many precocious young women these days, she seemed both serious and playful, elusive and direct.

So, Señor Ben—what must you ask me?

To start, where did you learn to work horses?

From my uncle Eduardo. He grew up on a hacienda near Matamoros, came north in his twenties. He showed me things.

How did you get that horse to accept you so quick?

Who knows? Horses pay attention, and know more than we think. Maybe he's just never been around a girl.

I sat and studied her. Then said Whatever you did it sure worked. But I didn't come to steal your secrets. When I asked if she wanted coffee, she beat me getting up, refilled my cup then served herself. Rosa went through the swinging door into the dining room to see what else the family might need.

Actually, I just wanted to see what you're about. What do you know about cattle?

Not near enough. I spent two summers with Eduardo, and we doctored and tagged and that kind of thing.

Did you ever pull a calf?

Several. They all lived.

What are your plans for the future?

I have no plans. One day at a time. Finding that horse yesterday was a start.

What do you call him?

Joker. Bromistar.

I complimented her on the name, then said if she wanted she might ride with us on the fall roundup in a couple weeks, maybe see how we did things.

Is that a job offer?

It might go that direction. Let's just see how you do. You made a pretty good impression on the boys.

Bunch a chatterboxes. But don't tell 'em I said so. With that she rose and held up her hand in farewell, then headed up the back stairs, but not before I caught the ghost of a smile curving past.

For a while then things seemed to change at the K-Bar. Estelle brought a new feeling to the place. As most attractive young women will, she brought promise and luster, a gleaming sense that anything was possible. Her attention and intelligence were like a spotlight that lit up whatever she turned to. Pretty soon there was a line of young cow hands hanging around her, ready with their offerings. The wildest was a shoebox piglet with red ribbon that she laughed and hugged, then handed back, saying This little one still needs her mama.

Even I wasn't immune, though I reined myself in, took the role of uncle protector. It appeared what I had was something she might need, since she sought me out, wanted to compare notes and see what I thought about things that mattered. I knew she was missing a father. For a while I even thought she might be trying to play matchmaker with her mother and me, though Rosa like her daughter also said One day at a time, which one sleepless night I recalled as the motto for Alcoholics Anonymous. But I could never seem to work it into polite conversation with either mother or daughter, so gave it up as none of my business.

Then came the fall roundup, with its planning all set for the push. I had the boys pull the chuck wagon out of the barn, sweep the mice and chickens out of the bed, grease the axles and stitch a couple spots on the canvas cover, check that all the nuts and pins were tight, then let Cooky direct them to load in the usual supplies, fill the water barrel, and with the grub safely stowed, load the boys' bedrolls in behind the seat. I gave Estelle a partner for the drive, Rusty, a seasoned hand with a little red in his beard but his hair mostly gray.

The morning we rode out, fog had settled in the lowlands, that made for a landscape of dreams. We could hardly see one another, and the fog muffled sounds, the creak and jingling, the click of hooves against stone. Then hills heaved up out of nowhere, menacing till the mist burned off.

The plan was to make eighteen miles the first day, then set up camp, so we could start herding first thing next morning. But for the morning fog the ride was mostly a picnic, starting jackrabbits and mule deer and other wildlife now and then as we climbed into the foothills, the boys playful, in high spirits. Someone spotted a small burrowing owl that flared up at our approach, and a couple of the boys gave chase till they lost it in some scrub along the creek.

Estelle couldn't help but be the center of the ride, with her Bromistar well-behaved, his head high. She had been working him with a saddle and blanket ever since that first day, an ancient patched Mexican rig with a horn big around as a fence post, that the boys studied but never said a word. A hand's gear was his own, not open for discussion except by invitation. And she never mentioned it.

We pushed hard, stopped half an hour for Cooky to pass around sandwiches, fruit and corn dodgers. With no problems we pressed on, and by nightfall were settled into the hands' favorite camp, the one called The Lookout. We got the fire going for Cooky, strung out a line for the remuda, fed and watered them, then dug out our bedrolls. It was a level patch of high ground, and in the fading light we could see mists far off settling into the valleys. Tomorrow would come early, and fall nights up here could be cold.

Cooky woke me with coffee at first light. Before that cup was gone everybody else was up rolling their bedding, some well into the dance of getting fed. I recruited a couple of good hands and set them up to ride fence at that end of the place, a couple miles further on. I gave them tools, spare wire and a plat map to mark any bad spots they couldn't fix, so we could come back with reinforcements and finish the job. I told them to find the far southwest corner, and work north. With a hundred-twelve odd miles of fence around the K-Bar we had to take every chance in good weather we might get.

Then it was flapjacks and sausage, and on with the drive. I set the hands up in groups of three, each with a trail boss, and gave the usual speech before we saddled up, every year the same. Try not to run the cattle. Don't run them just for fun. Keep mamas and calves together. Be calm. Dig them out of scrub and arroyos where they like to hide. Keep them ahead of you, don't let any sneak by. We're gonna round them up at Adobe Flats a mile to the east. If your horse comes up lame, get a buddy to ride back and fetch you another from the string. Tie your lame one and pick it up at the end of the day. Remember, the more we get done now, the less to do later on.

And with that we were off. I was on Jericho, the big sweet paint gelding that had been my number one pony since Apache. He was surefooted, good at cutting cows, with no bad habits to speak of. I worked him pretty hard but treated him right, and he came up shining. By the end of a day I didn't mind stepping down to let us both climb a hill and catch our breath.

As for Estelle, I smiled in her direction, though we hadn't spoken in days. I'd put her with Rusty and one other hand but mostly let her be, to see what she'd do with all the work going on. If her effect on the boys would prove a help or hindrance. If she would find her place. The cows were going to take our full attention, and she didn't need an earful of expectations before the show even started.

That first day was hard, with more bruises and spills than we commonly get. One horse slipped off a steep trail, down a rocky gulch backwards, broke a hind leg and had to be put down on the spot. The rider got banged up, and needed help to get his rig off the dead horse, then walked back to camp for another mount, but a couple hours later was back at it and fine. Nobody wanted to take time off for lunch, though Cooky came out to find us with more sandwiches and fruit and thermoses of coffee, and made us stop a minute.

As for Estelle, she was already showing more cowboy than most. Her horse was still a little green and rough, but willing, and would likely be fine. She knew not to lead cattle, but move alongside, nudge, give them time to react and accept. She had a calm about her, and made no startling moves.

By sundown we had rounded up roughly 200 head. I made night assignments to keep the cattle together on the Flats, in four-hour shifts. Then we left three hands riding herd, and picked our way back to camp in the gathering dark.

Bixler the Cooky was fixing steak and biscuits and beans. In short order the boys slipped their saddles off, fed and watered their ponies, then got into the grub line. They were so hungry supper didn't take long. Then around the fire the boys got into their blankets and bags, for all their exhaustion too wound up to sleep. We had brought tents, but hadn't pitched any, since the night was clear, the rains still a month off.

Pretty soon a handful started clanking their coffee cups on the rocks, chanting my name. Ben Ben Ben Ben. I stepped into the firelight and said What's all the ruckus?

One of them shouted Tell us a story!

You sure that's what you want? When they answered with cheers, I said Well okay then.

So I told them the story that no one but Len Dawes and the Kendricks

family had ever heard. Once upon a time out in Fresno was a boy. With a
father raised on a small farm in the foothills up above Merced, always said
he knew how to crank a shovel and which end to milk a chicken. Mostly
liked the life, but hated how things broke down at harvest, right when you
had most need of them. With his dad no hand at machinery, plagued by
doubt and fear of failure. Which may be why he got good at body work,
never lifted the hood or crawled under a car if he could help it. He had one
guy in his body shop, Brad Fuller, who was the real mechanic, that they
kept busy fixing the junkers they patched up, that were the backbone of the
business.

Then his Dad got run down by a train at a grade crossing on the way
home to the boy's eleventh birthday, with a new bike in the trunk. A faulty
signal arm never came down, no bells or lights. How we had stale birthday
cake next morning for breakfast, then I was farmed out to relatives in San
Angelo, got into it with a cousin-in-law when I was seventeen. Him pulling
his belt out, me throwing punches and a dishpan full of crockery. How I
run off but got lucky, got onto a ranch, then another, then found my way
onto this one. How I got my legs under me as a cowboy. The couple good
horses I'd had. My love life, such as it was, and how that worked out. About
the little ranch I'd bought from a sweet old couple and still have, about
an hour's drive away. How it had been some years since I'd gotten serious
about any woman, how I'd moved back into the bunkhouse here for a little
chin-music after nightfall, what folks like to call company. Every now and
again I'd say Stop me if you heard this. But by now the silence was like
velvet. It felt like we could hear whippoorwills and crickets out along the
Milky Way. No one was asleep, no one even looked sleepy.

Then I had a thought, stepped back from the fire to pull a full bottle
out of my saddle bag, uncorked and poured myself a splash, handed it to
the nearest cowboy and said Pass it around. Make sure everyone gets a taste.

By then there was practically nothing left to the story, no real end.
How Len Dawes the best cowboy I'd ever known stepped down as boss a
few years back, who'd be here this minute if he wasn't nursing his dying
sister, how the Kendricks family asked me to step in. So here we are, and
the reason why we're here will come around to bite us bright and early. So
I bid you all a good night. And remember, shake out your boots before you

step in 'em.

And with that I tipped up my cup, and so did the rest. Then stepped out of the firelight, sat down and pulled off my boots. As I lay back to spread myself around, Estelle bent over, squeezed my arm and whispered Gracias. Though she didn't say for what.

Next morning arrived in a hurry. First to be fed were two boys that took the day shift with the herd on the Flats, who rode out to spell the night riders come in for breakfast and a nap. Then while some were still eating, we gathered around the map, and talked about where the rest of the cattle might be. I shuffled up the groups from yesterday, and sent each out to scout a likely canyon. I took charge of one myself, saddled up Jericho and headed out. Estelle wound up riding with a different group, heading north, that I didn't expect to see back until dark.

The second day was harder than the first. Climbing into higher, rougher country, with more scrub and rock outcroppings, more hidey-holes. We dug out a few big old animals missed last spring, that didn't care to be driven, that we had to work in pairs. By the end of the day, the hands and their horses were shambling and stumbling. But no one had gotten hurt, and as we worked our way back to Adobe Flats, spirits were high. The total herd seemed huge, and must have been near 600 as the boys wheeled them in the dusty twilight, to stir the newcomers in, calm them down. Watching them wheel felt like a slow quiet prayer.

As we rode up to The Lookout, I could hear Bixler the Cooky off in the dark somewhere fussing, clanging pans, and soon knew why. There were a couple fancy new horses in camp, tied at the end of the string, and there were the newlywed owners, Lionel and Cynthia Kendricks, warming their hands by the fire. Which was a smoky mess, with Cooky barbecuing ribs, slathering on the sauce, and stirring four big Dutch ovens, two with chilies, beans and rice, the other two with potato, onion and cheese casseroles. I hopped down to greet them, said What a pleasure, too bad we can't show you the herd right now, but you'll see in the morning. I knew Lionel had never ridden a roundup since he went off to college, but kept mum, just made them welcome. We had no folding chairs, but we could offer them supper and shelter for the night, and I could see they had brought bedrolls.

So I had a couple of the boys pitch them a tent, and gave them each a flashlight and a roll of toilet paper, and shined them the way to the outhouse.
And slipped Lionel that other bottle I had planned to share with the hands.

The barbecue proved to be a real treat. Cooky was actually blushing in
the firelight from the compliments. And I was proud how well the hands
behaved. We dug out several lanterns to string overhead so we could see
what we were eating, which made things kind of festive. There could have
been an awkward moment when Cynthia saw Estelle in line for supper, but
Estelle stepped up to shake her hand, asked about her ride, and admired her
new Western saddle. With the attentive greeting, Cynthia was relaxed and
beaming.

After supper a couple of the boys played some tunes on banjo and
harmonica. First some slow mournful ones, like The Streets of Laredo.
But when they started in on Buffalo Gal Won't You Come Out Tonight,
Lionel jumped up and two-stepped his lady round the fire, and the boys
sang along in their raggedy way, and at the end gave a thunderous ovation,
whooping till the canyons rang. After that I watched several of the boys try
to pull Estelle up to dance, but she wisely refused. There should be only one
belle at this ball.

It was a high old time, with several other dance tunes everyone could
sing and swing to, but then simmered down. Cooky passed around some
cookies he'd baked, then the hands got into their bedrolls. Lionel and Cynthia bid us all good night, and went to their tent, and next thing anybody
knew Cooky was handing me coffee, and there was blood on the rim of the
world.

After breakfast I shuffled up the trail groups again but this time left
myself out, figured I needed to spend time with Lionel and Cynthia. The
drive to come would likely be more nightmare than dream, a slow messy
noisy thing that would take all our attention.

Cynthia got up first, came out to the fire, stepped close and warmed
her hands. She seemed in fine spirits even before the coffee, full of questions
and comments. She said she'd ridden to hounds and competed in jumping
and dressage, but had never herded cattle, and was astonished at how smart
these working horses were. I told her about an old friend who'd worked
hay fields in Arizona, where on account of the heat they had to mow in the

dark, and the teams of horses pulled their mowers around the fields in the moonlight without anyone driving them. Teamsters waited at the four corners with lanterns to guide them through the turns, and the teams mowed on till they stopped at the center, waiting for teamsters to unhitch and lead them in.

Then Lionel was with us, set for the day in his big white Stetson. We freshened our coffee, while Cooky fried us some flapjacks and sausage and eggs. I told them where the hands were, what they'd be doing, and suggested we ride over and see the herd. While we were finishing breakfast, I told them a little about the spot where we were, The Lookout. It was the best view off the ranch to an ancient migration trail heading south, and the only archaeological site so far found on the place. Every now and again a native wanderer or two might appear out of the South, passing through. Dried chilis and beans and tobacco might be shared, .22 shells or twine, or whatever else they might have need of, that we had. This flat spot with its grand overlook had been a campsite long before the ranch, and a university researcher doing some kind of survey had gathered up a heap of bones and shards, likely evidence this fire pit had been in use for eleven or twelve thousand years. There was a good spring hidden at a shady spot in the rocks just to the east, that was always full spring and fall, never known to go dry. The spring was boxed in by sandstone building blocks like those used in Anasazi pueblos. The ranch had always maintained three campsites, each with a wood pile and an outhouse, here at its far end, for roundups. Adobe Flats had been an early Spanish homestead, the biggest clearing this end of the spread. It had never been fenced, and was abandoned before Texans and their railroads reached this far west. There were only a couple low adobe walls left, that we'd improvised into a stock pen.

As I described the place and its history, Lionel kept a hard eye on me, that I couldn't read. Had I got something wrong? He'd kept his distance from ranch operations for years, so might not have heard all of this. Or might not like hearing it now, in front of his new wife. Or maybe he had other fish to fry.

With that we saddled up and headed out to see the herd. I noticed that they packed everything they brought, so would probably be heading home. Then over a rise up ahead Cynthia and Lionel reined up, and in a

moment I drew even. And there it was, a vast slow wheel of bawling cattle
a mile across, milling clockwise, by now a thousand head or more. Hard
to say with the dust. There were a few hands rounding them, and several
more driving cattle down out of the hills. I had that prayer feeling again.
Cynthia's eyes were sparkling. I asked what she thought, and she said it was
grand, like nothing she'd ever seen. Lionel was still distracted, not really enjoying the spectacle, all the work and skills in motion. Here was the K-Bar's
whole reason for existing, at a glance. Then all at once Estelle flashed by on
her pony, and Lionel grumbled What's she doing here?

Maybe he just forgot he'd seen her last night around camp, or had never even noticed her. But something was wrong, that I needed to get hold of.
I waited until they'd seen enough and turned to go, then we picked our way
down to lower country. When we were on a level, I stopped in a little grove,
climbed down and tied Jericho to a branch, made as if to tighten his cinch,
and offered to check theirs as well. While we were stretching our legs, Cynthia said When I saw that girl Estelle, I couldn't help but think that's what
I'd love to do. Help out on roundups, if you thought I'd be of use. I told
her You'd surely be welcome, and you could pick it up in no time. Half the
work is a good willing horse that knows cattle. At that Lionel practically let
out a moan.

I asked him Was there something wrong? Avoiding my eyes, he looked
off and blurted out, To tell you the truth, we've been thinking of selling the
place. Thought we oughta ride out and see it while it's still like this.

What do you mean?

Before it all changes. I stepped around to look him full in the face,
couldn't help it. It felt like the ground had just opened up. I always thought
I knew what his problem was, but didn't really. It wasn't my place, and
wasn't my say-so. Not about what mattered, who and what stayed or went. I
might be ramrod, but had been fooling myself.

Before what changes?

Ben, you know good an' well what I mean. This whole ranch has been
a dream, livin' in the past for fifty years, Dyin' for as long as you and I been
alive. Hell, you still got Cooky drivin' a chuck wagon team on these windy
little trails.

Pays for itself, don't it.

Just barely. We can't be runnin' a rest home for broken-down cowboys.

I had to set him straight. Said That herd up there would bring upwards of a million and a half just as it stands. A million in good breeding stock, the finest hereabouts. And the yearlings there now that were last winter's calves will bring their half a million at market. When the heifers we breed calve in the spring that'll be another half a million to market next fall. It's not like the wages are eatin' us up. Or expenses. We've still got another cutting of hay set to bale by first frost.

I know it runs good, thanks to you, and it's what the boys think they all want, but maybe not what we need. Ben, I'm grateful for your work and your thoughts. But Cynthia and I need to figure how we want to live, and what we want to do. This may be our one chance to make a change before it's too late. It may turn out we'll find someone to buy the place, who sees eye to eye with you. But the way the ranching business is these days, more likely not.

And with that, he swung up into the saddle. Cynthia avoided my eye, and climbed up too. So I mounted Jericho and said I'd ride with them a little further on, till they were on the trail for home. Lionel started to say they'd find their way, but didn't fight me, even seemed relieved, especially since I had no more to say. The starch had gone completely out of me.

An hour later we got to the fork that met the main trail. As we were saying goodbye, Lionel said By the way, tell that gal, Rosa's daughter, I don't want her hanging round the boys. Distracting 'em. I tried not to stare, said I'd invited her along on this roundup to see could she make it as a cowhand, maybe offer her a job. And what's your opinion, he said. I said She's a hell of a hand with the horses, and has worked cows as much as most of the boys. There's no doubt they've accepted her. And she more than holds her own. I really been thinkin' how the place needs her more than she needs us, how she'd be the first regular woman cowhand in these parts. She might kinda be the future. That might be worthwhile to offer a hand.

Lionel turned in his saddle to look at me close. So did Cynthia. They didn't look at each other, but both nodded to me. Lionel raised his hand, said Later, and they rode on.

I climbed back up to Adobe Flats, watched the cattle wheel a few minutes, felt their quiet power in motion, then headed north to find cows. Work is about the only medicine for a heavy heart. An ornery wild cow or steer won't let you be, and a cow pony will soon set you straight.

That night would be our last at The Lookout. Maybe our last ever. Tomorrow we'd move the herd north to The Box, a dead-end canyon where decades back we'd strung fence and a gate across the mouth, that would let the boys get some sleep before we started the long drive home.

Turned out I found more cows than I bargained for, on a tight mountain trail with a steep drop-off to the north. I heard their distant thunder before I saw a thing, crowded Jericho to the inside wall, and reined in with seconds to spare. Here they come, twenty-two head, big, rank and wild, with a bull herding them, clattering down the trail. And behind them, right on their heels, was that girl's rangy liver-colored horse Bromistar. I whirled Jericho around, snatched my lariat, snapped a loop at the horse's head and missed, tossed again and caught him. Then we slowed to a stop. I stepped down and approached Bromistar, looked him over. He still had Estelle's Mexican saddle on, but was missing one of his reins, maybe torn away when he stepped on it coming down the mountain. Or maybe it broke and startled her. I talked to him, touched and calmed him. He didn't limp, and seemed to have escaped without a scratch.

We rode back up the trail, pushed up through gathering clouds, picking our way, calling her name now and then. I didn't want to look over the edge but forced myself, and saw nothing. Then around a tight bend near the top there she was, sitting in the trail in sunlight with one boot and sock off, her long foot red and swollen. I couldn't see her face. Her hair was loose, a shining tent around her shoulders. I stepped down, tied Jericho to some sage, and knelt to feel if her ankle was broken. Luckily it didn't seem to be. So I took off my neckerchief, rolled it up and showed her how to tie her ankle, to immobilize the sprain. So far Estelle hadn't said a thing, just shook her hair back and tucked it under her collar, that let me see a fat tear welling in one eye.

I dug through my saddlebags for the hank of cotton clothesline I keep for such things, cut and tied a length onto Bromistar's bridle. When we'd worked her boot on, I pulled her to her feet and lifted her into the saddle. I didn't bother to ask could she ride, or say anything else till we got turned around, heading down the mountain with me in the lead to catch anything else busted loose.

As we dropped down through the clouds, at last she spoke. Said I didn't want you to see me like that. I said Let's just be glad you're all right. You know that old saying, There's never a horse that couldn't be rode, never a cowboy that couldn't be throwed. Just then Bromistar snorted, shook his head, and she laughed.

Then she said He was just doing what I wanted, heading those cows. One turn he just ran out from under me. I said That's how it is with no room to work. But that's a nice bunch, and we'll catch 'em down on the level. A little herd all to themselves, they won't scatter.

Then the talk moved on to other things. On impulse I swore her to secrecy, then told her what the owners had said. As cowhands will, I told her what made sense and what didn't, how Cynthia had suddenly opened up to what the ranch was about, wanted to help herd cattle, just as Lionel was pulling away, thinking this was his chance to escape. Then I told Estelle what I'd told them, how she fit in, how she'd make a good hand, the first real cowgirl in these parts. Then said Things at the K-Bar are wobbly just now. But know you always got a job with me.

She reined in her horse. I stopped and over my shoulder said What. She said I got a notion Cynthia might like the place better than she lets on at the moment, maybe better than she knows. She'll be the one to decide, not him. Maybe I'll take her riding a few times, and see what develops. Just give her time.

Then still behind me she said, You wanta see something? If you never tell a soul. I slowed and turned. She took that tin out of her hip pocket, grinned and said Here's my secret, one anyhow, and handed me a warm mint. Cinnamon. Bromistar nosed after her hand, so she leaned down to give him one too.

We soon caught up with that rank bunch and with no trouble rounded them toward the herd. As we drove those cows down into that huge wheel of cattle turning clockwise in the sun, its dusty prayer swirling up, I recalled something I'd meant to tell Cynthia and Lionel. How merry-go-rounds mostly go counterclockwise—like horses at the race track, and

like the faithful at Mecca. You know why? She turned to smile at me, as if
she was born knowing. She said 'Cause we love how we seem to go faster,
against the spin of the world.

Author's Note

There are a handful of Texas ranches the size of the fictional K-Bar, and several larger, from half a million to near a million acres, bigger than Rhode Island, that still employ cowhands on horseback, breed and raise grass-fed beef the old way. These are self-contained weather-beaten little worlds where change comes slowly, at the speed of mounted riders. Their methods may not turn a quick profit, but the land has long been deeded and handed down, and is not depleted by over-grazing. We could easily imagine folks might still act on the urge to follow the seasons and herds in another hundred years, as they have the past hundred and fifty, weather and humans permitting.

But the trappings of fiction can mask sterner realities. A branch of the author's Ulster Scot family that settled in North Carolina in 1730 found its way to the Texas frontier after fighting in the Revolution and the War of 1812. His great-great grandmother waltzed with Sam Houston at the Governor's first inaugural ball. His great-grandfather, a saddle-maker, died in a gunfight while serving as acting sheriff of Wills Point, Texas the day after Christmas, 1892. More recently the author met an old Texas rancher who spoke of being rescued from a muddy ditch by an old smart cow, when she was a tiny girl.

As for the author, he has pitch-forked hundreds of tons of manure, strung miles of fence, and herded all manner of cattle as the weather circled and pounced. He worked on traditional Midwestern farms, around animals large and small, studying their ways, exploring the roots of his country-raised parents in Kentucky and Indiana. A teacher and writer about matters rural, he has published eleven other books. He did know a tall red horse early on, that faithfully carried him far without a misstep. A few other horses threw him, but he got back on.

www.ingramcontent.com/pod-product-compliance
Lightning Source LLC
Chambersburg PA
CBHW071013180726
48291CB00004B/1447

9 781885 210333